A GANGSTER'S MELODY
A Novel by Sean A. Wright

Copyright 2011
Just Wright Publications
Printed in USA

All rights reserved. No part of this book may be reproduced or transmitted in any form or by other means, electronic or mechanical, including photocopying, recording, or by any information storage and retrieval system without the expressed written permission from the author, except for the inclusion of brief quotes for review.

This work is a work of fiction. Any resemblance to actual events or person(s) living or deceased is strictly coincidental. All characters, incidents and dialog are the product of the author's imagination and are in no way tied to real events or people.

Cover Design: Junnita Jackson
Front Cover Model: Melinda Laureano
Back Cover Model: Orlando Laureano
Interior Design: Msbgraphix.net

ISBN: 1466379707

Dedication:

To the greatest parents in the world Larry and Janice Wright, I love you and thank you for giving me years of wisdom, guidance, near perfect parenting and most importantly "THE GIFT OF LIFE".

To my siblings; Kasaan , Jermaine, Rikki, Karim, I love you all. I couldn't ask to be a big brother and example to a better set of siblings. (I could ask but who would listen)

To my children; Michael and DeSeanique, I love you both unconditionally and when it's all said and done, I do all of this for you. You both are my sole reason for living and grinding every day. Daddy loves you.

ACKNOWLEDGEMENTS:

There are so many people I want to thank for so many reasons, but I'm sure I won't be able to single out everyone. So if I don't mention your name but you know you deserve to see it, just know you are in my heart and words can't express all that I feel anyway.

Mom- With everything you have been through and all that you have overcome in your life. I use you as my muse. And when I paint my portrait of determination it will come out to look just like you.

Dad- All the years that you worked double and triple shifts for 7days straight just to provide for us has paid off. You taught me that if you want something bad enough then you have to work extra hard. And to prove that I listen when I get rich off of this book I'm buying stock in MECHANICAL SCARECROWS!

Kasaan- Thanks for teaching me what you know about the book game. (shorty can't eat no books)

Rikki- Thanks for all of the support, and late night talks. I am sooo proud of you.

Jermaine- Thanks for always keeping it real with me..keep doin ya thing.

Karim- (knock knock)- Thanks for always being there whenever I needed to talk or vent. Our bond is crazy.

Brittani Williams- Thank you for teaching me ALL that I know about the literary game. You gave me the hope ,confidence, and know how to take this thing all the way. All of your help, wisdom and guidance will not go unrecognized. I owe you…and I thank you!

Damon Hasan Johnson- (my brother till the end) I thank you for being my right hand man since 4th grade. We have come a very long way. We have beaten the odds and statistics. A friendship/brotherhood like our can never be altered or replaced. Thank you for teaching me all that I know about BUSINESS period and most of all thanks for being my friend.

Shaneekwa Smith- Thanks for not paying your Worldcom bill. 10+ years later look at us now. Thank you for always having my back. Our bond will never be understood or broken.

Uncle Danny- Thank you for always having my back. You are the world's Greatest Godfather.

Uncle Phil, Aunt Robin, Nicole, & Shaun- It took me till I was 38 m*&^%ckin years old but I did it.

To the **Rockaway Blvd and the 140th street crew-** I made it ya'll!

Rhawnie Davis- Thanks for teaching me all the things that I should have already known. We have been through some wars, but hey that's what FRIENDS do. (there..I finally said it) you cannot get rid of SEAN-A-THAN..lol

Felicia Hunt-WOW! (need I say more?)

To my friends and fans I thank you all for your support.

Melinda Laureano- Thanks for posing for my cover. This is only the beginning. I told you I got you.

Junnita Jackson- Thanks for giving me the best cover ever. Thanks for dealing with my late night jitters, last minute changes and phone calls. Thanks for getting team Sean off and running.

To my man Fred Lee- thanks for holding me down Bee..lol

And a BIG thank you to **Nicole Shelton** for seeing and believing in my vision.

To anyone I may have missed, I will be bringing the world years of my literary gift so I will catch you in books to come. Just know that you are not forgotten.

Thank You!

Prologue

June 25th 2006 was the night that would change my life forever. Mama and me were at the dinner table eating alone as usual, because daddy was working late again at the office. Tonight I was really enjoying dinner. Not just because mama had fixed my favorite dish of fried chicken with mashed potatoes, collard greens, corn bread and gravy, but more so because this was the rare occasion when I actually had someone to eat with. See, daddy was an executive at the Marketing Firm he worked for that on occasion would cause him to be stuck at the office very late and mama would often go over to Ms Gloria's house for a night of gossip and late night spades games. This neglect caused me to end up home alone often and daddy didn't like that. He especially didn't like trying to contact mama on her cell phone and her not picking up, and he hated calling Ms. Gloria's house and her saying mama wasn't there.

Most times daddy would make it home from a long night at the office way before mama would make it home from Ms. Gloria's house. Those antics would often cause heated arguments that lasted until the wee hours of the morning. I hated to hear those arguments and I hated to pick sides because I loved my parents both equally and unconditionally. But daddy was right. Some of mama's actions were inappropriate and unbecoming of a good wife.

I mean, in daddy's defense, he did work all day and all night at the firm so that we could have the finer things in life so that mama wouldn't have to work. Mama on the other hand stayed home all day, watched reality T.V. and spent daddy's money. But I guess that's what divas do. Mama and I were enjoying our conversation about me being so good at doing hair and how I wanted to open up my own salon one day when daddy burst through the front door yelling and screaming about mama cheating on him. He was in a venomous rage and he smelled like a liquor store.

Daddy had accused mama of cheating before, but this time was different. Without much warning he smacked mama out of the chair and dragged her kicking and screaming into the bedroom. I was in total shock. As far back as I could remember daddy had never raised his hand to mama. This was all happening so fast I had no time to react. I just sat there speechless. By the time I snapped out of my trance and ran to the bedroom door it was locked and I could only hear him beating her savagely on the other side of it. I cried and begged for him to stop while I banged on the door. After what seemed like an eternity I heard a gunshot, and then there was an eerie silence. The door opened and daddy came out with a gun in his hand drenched in blood. He walked passed me and I ran into the room. My worst fears were confirmed. There was my mother, her beautiful Hispanic skin battered and bruised with a hole in her heart from the .45 that daddy kept in the house for protection. I screamed to the top of my lungs and ran into the living room where my father, my hero sat there with the gun in his hand and a cigarette dangling from his lips. He turned, looked at me with tears in his eyes and said, "I'm so sorry baby."

Before I could reach him he put the gun to his head and pulled the trigger...

A FRESH START

I was awakened yet again by the sound of the infant baby next to me screaming to the top of her lungs. I had been on the Greyhound for hours now and when this lady and her baby got on in Cleveland I knew it was going to be an even longer ride to Baltimore. I had never been on a Greyhound before and my first trip was proving to be a horrible one.

The lady, who just happened to sit next to me, had to be all of 400 lbs so when she sat down she inadvertently pinned me up against the window. And then the constant crying of her baby made matters even worse. Now don't get me wrong, I have nothing against big people, and I love babies but this was ridiculous. I managed to free one of my arms to use the pre-paid cell phone given to me by Mrs. Gloria to use for the trip.

After my parents' funeral I was left with a decision to make. It was either go to Puerto Rico and stay with my mother's side of the family or go to Baltimore and stay with my dad's mother. I barely knew either side of the family. Since they both lived so far away, I hardly ever got to see them. I mean, an occasional summer here and there but that was about it. I never really understood why the closeness wasn't there but I think it had something to do with the disapproval of my mom and dad's marriage. I was actually born in Baltimore, but after my birth, then the marriage, from what I am told all hell broke loose. So when daddy's firm asked him to take the job in the small town of Marion, Ohio he figured what the hell? I wasn't old enough to be in school yet, and I was too young to have any friends to miss. So he packed us up and moved us to a place where we could be one big happy family just my daddy, my mama, and me.

I had chosen to move back to Baltimore. I figured since I was much older now, and I was raised in the suburbs of Marion where there is absolutely nothing to do, the live streets of Baltimore is where I wanted to be. I had been trying to call my grandmother periodically since I left Marion to confirm that she would be picking me up, and also just to let her know that I was okay. But each time I called she either didn't pick up or she was very short winded with me. So here I was calling again to let her know that I would finally be pulling into the bus station in 10 minutes but yet again I only got her voice mail. *'Oh well'* I thought, I hope she is there on time. I didn't even know what she looked like. The whole situation didn't sit well with me but it was too late to turn back now and besides, it was time that I got to know my dad's family.

When I got off the bus I looked around and didn't see anyone who looked familiar to me. I called my grandmother's cell phone again, and again it just rang and went to voice mail. I also called her house and still no answer. Damn. What was I going to do now? I had no choice but to sit on a nearby bench and wait for her to show up. As time went by I saw people slowly starting to vacate the area with friends and family that were waiting to pick them up. I had been there for 30 minutes and still no word from my grandmother. Then, just when I was about to call her again I saw an elderly woman that looked just like my daddy. She was standing near a car with another elderly man. That has got to be her I thought to myself. But what if I was wrong? No. I couldn't be wrong. She looked too much like my daddy. In any event I had to give it a chance.

I grabbed my suitcase and walked over to her. She was so engulfed in her conversation with her man-friend that she never saw me approaching. I was sud-

A Gangster's Melody   11

denly overcome with a feeling of uncontrollable nerves. I stuttered as I tapped her on the shoulder.

"Uh, excuse me. Grandma Bell?" she turned around with a scowl on her face that would scare anybody away.

"Tiffany?" She kind of barked at me.

"Yes maam. Hey grandma longtime no see." I said reaching out to hug her. She ignored the gesture and looked at her watch.

"Well it's about damn time you got here. You know how long I been out here waiting on you?" Damn. She was coming at me like I drove the bus or like I wasn't waiting on her too.

"Grandma, I was over there waiting on you for like 30 minutes. I didn't even know you were over here. I have been calling you all day and..."

She cut me off. "Look child, just get in the car. And stop with all the back talk. I'm already late putting my dinner on fooling with you." She turned to her man friend

"Rufus. Put yo eyes back in ya head and help with the suitcase so we can get on out of here."

He extended his hand. "Hello little lady, how are you? My name is Rufus. I'm a friend of your grand-mama's."

I shook his hand. "Hello sir. My name is Tiffany."

He was reluctant to let my hand go. "Well hello Tiffany. How are you?" He said with a sly smile showing his one gold tooth surrounded by empty spaces where the others used to be.

"Rufus put the damn bags in the car." Grandma yelled. This was going to be very interesting.

As we drove through the streets of Baltimore it didn't take long for me to realize that I was a long way from Marion, Ohio. The streets were so busy and every block was so congested. I had never seen so many

12 *Sean Wright*

people clustered together in one area in my life. I saw everything from young girls jumping double dutch, to two grown women fighting in the middle of the street.

A little further down, I saw pimps and prostitutes. I then saw a man leaned over with spit hanging out of his mouth and he appeared to be asleep while he was standing up. But I couldn't understand how he could lean over so far without falling, especially while he was asleep. And then just like that. He woke up, stood up stra'ight, wiped his mouth and staggered up the street. I would learn later that he was what is commonly known as a dope fiend. My last show before we turned onto Mama Bell's block was a boy who couldn't have been no older than sixteen pull a gun out on grown man and yell out "Nigga do I gotta kill you to get my fucking money?" I was amazed because all of this was done in broad daylight and the other people just kept going on about their business like they didn't see anything. Even Mama Bell and Rufus just kept driving unfazed. This must have been the norm around here. What did I get myself into?

When we pulled up to Mama Belle's house nothing really looked too familiar. I mean, the last time I was here was years ago. I was only around 7 or 8 I think. Mama Belle's house sat in the middle of a pretty decent looking block compared to what I had seen in Baltimore so far. She owned a two-story house that was green and white. In the front yard there were porcelain figurines and fake pink flamingos for some reason. There was a porch with a rocking chair and wind chimes that hung from the porch roof. The house was in need of a good painting. The paint was chipped and looked like it hadn't been done over since the house was built. But hey, who was I to complain? This was my new home. At least until I could get settled, go to

A Gangster's Melody

school, find a job and save up to move out. I really couldn't wait to get into the salon business.

My father used to order me fashion and hair magazines and between the magazines and music videos I knew Baltimore females had some of the best hairstyles I had ever seen. Yeah. They shit was tight, and I couldn't wait to be held responsible for the hair do's that would be the talk of the town. When I got inside the house I stopped and looked around. Things were really looking different. Everywhere I turned there was some sort of religious symbol. Either a Bible or a cross hanging up, there was even a tapestry of the last supper.

On the hallway wall there was the one poem that every black family had on the wall. Yeah, you guessed it. "Footprints". Mama Belle must have noticed the confused look on my face.

"Yeah. Things look a lot different since the last time you were here huh? First room on the left is yours. Everything you need is on the bed." Mr. Rufus followed me into the bedroom with my suitcase.

The room was unbearably small. It wasn't even the size of a full bedroom. It was hardly furnished. There was a small nightstand that was lopsided so it tilted back and forth. Against the wall was a small dresser and for some reason the bottom drawer was missing. There was no T.V. and the bed was only a twin size and that barely fit in the room. There wasn't even a closet. I was definitely not used to living like this but it would have to do for now. I looked on the bed and noticed a washcloth, towel, bar of soap and a newspaper.

I yelled out into the hallway "Hey Grandma, what's the newspaper for?" Grandma came out of the kitchen and headed to my room.

"It's so you can get your tail up in the morning and look for a job, that's what it's for. Now you family and

14   *Sean Wright*

all, but ain't no free rides around here." I couldn't believe what I was hearing.

"But grandma, I just got here." She put her hands on her hips.

"Yeah I know, and the sooner you get to work, the sooner you can help with the lights, gas and groceries. Now that's the end of it. Go get washed up for dinner."

I rolled my eyes and closed my door, then let out a deep sigh and plopped down on my bed. It was all hard and shit. I started to unpack my clothes but then decided to do it later. All I wanted to do at this point was to take a shower and relax. I grabbed my nightclothes and headed to the bathroom. The bathroom was covered in blue wallpaper and it had matching shower curtains. I went to put my toothbrush in the toothbrush holder on the sink and I jumped back in a mixture of excitement and fear. Sitting right there on the sink in a jar of water was Mama Belle's dentures. They scared the shit out of me. I smiled and got prepared for my shower.

Once inside the shower I let the hot water pour over my head as I leaned my head up against the porcelain tiles. While the hot soothing water poured over my body I became lost in my own thoughts and all I could do was think about mama and daddy and how much I missed them. I was also a little angry because they left me. They left me all alone. I broke down crying right there in the shower and silently cried out for my mother and father.

After I got out of the shower and put on my nightclothes. I brushed my teeth and headed back to my room. When I got back to my room I reached in my bag and unpacked two candles. I placed them on the night stand and lit them both. I then got on my knees and said my nightly prayer.

A Gangster's Melody   15

Each night since my parent's death I prayed that god would keep them safe, I prayed that I would be with them again one day, and I always ended the prayer wishing that their deaths were just a bad dream and that I would wake up from it. When the prayer was finished I crossed my heart and looked up into the sky.

"Good night mommy and daddy. I love you." I looked up and saw Mamma Belle standing in the door just watching me.

"C'mon and get to the table, dinner is ready."

"If it's okay with you Grandma, I'll skip dinner."

"Well suit ya'self, but if you ain't gonna' eat you need to carry your tail to bed. I've got you set up with a friend of the church for an interview tomorrow down at his diner. Now the job is practically yours, he just wants to meet you. So wear something nice and try not to mess this up." She turned on her heels and closed the door without even saying good night. I don't know what the problem was, but I was definitely not feeling the love. I prayed things would get greater later.

WELCOME TO THE HOOD

When I woke up the next morning I realized I had kicked the covers off of me during my night of restless sleep. I rolled over and was frightened by the sight of Mr. Rufus standing over me. I screamed in shock and quickly tried to cover myself.

"Mr. Rufus." At the same time Mama Belle walked into the room. Noticing that I was half naked with her man friend in the room she blew her top.

"Mr. Rufus my ass. If you don't put some damn clothes on I'll come over there and smack the shit out of you girl."

I tried to defend myself. "But grandma." But she wouldn't hear me out.

"But grandma my ass. Get yo fast hot ass up and get dressed."

I just sat there in a state of shock.

"Now Tiffany." she screamed to the top of her old lungs. Then her and that perverted ass Mr. Rufus closed the door and left.

"Ugghh" I screamed almost to the top of my lungs. I wasn't even here a full 24 hours yet and this shit was getting real tired, real fast. I took care of my morning hygiene and rummaged through my clothes to see what I could where to a job interview. I had never been on one before so I was like a fish out of water. After what seemed like hours I decided on a pair of black Roc-A-Wear jeans and red and black and red stretch Roc-A-Wear pullover top to match. On my feet I decided to put on a pair of red heels that I had. I don't remember where I got them from but I hardly every wore them because I never really went anywhere when I was back at home.

A Gangster's Melody 17

After I got dressed I combed my hair and put it in a long ponytail that stopped at the middle of my back. I didn't have a mirror to double check myself so I would just have to trust the fact that I knew how to dress. I yelled into the hallway to let Mama Belle know I was ready. She advised me that she was too, so we left. We rode in silence as Mama Belle played gospel music all the way to the diner.

When we pulled up to the diner she gave me the following instructions. "Now you go in there and ask for Jimmy. Tell him I sent you. She looked me up and down and then continued, "By the way you are dressed, you should have no problem getting the job," She said sarcastically. "I'll be back to get you when you are done. Just call the house."

I got out of the car and looked myself up and down to see if I could notice any flaws in my attire and to be totally honest I couldn't find anything wrong. I mean okay so maybe my jeans were a little form fitting but they weren't tight at all. I could still pinch and pull the fabric away from my legs and ass. And my shirt had no control over the way that my breasts were perfectly formed. I mean, I may not have been dressed to interview for a corporate position but I wasn't dressed for an escort service either. I looked up from my self-examination

"Mama Bell I just want to thank you..." I never got a chance to finish the sentence. She peeled off from the curb like she had just robbed a bank. I just watched in frustration as her green Cadillac got smaller going down the block. I pulled myself together and prepared to enter the building.

The diner was named Jimmy's Place. And maybe I shouldn't call it a diner. That would give you the misconception that it was some small greasy spoon hole in the wall. This place was more of a full-blown restaurant. It was black brick with gold writing and gold light post outside. It almost didn't fit in with the rest of the buildings on the block. Jimmy's Place was very elegant on the outside.

When I walked in all eyes were automatically on me and I could feel it. I walked up to the front counter and cleared my throat to take the man's attention off of my breast and have it focused on my face.

"Excuse me. I'm looking for Jimmy." I stated. Before the perverted older man could respond, a tap on the shoulder startled me. When I turned around I was met by a tall chocolate skinned man. He stood about 6 feet 3 inches tall. And although he looked to be around fifty or so he had a very muscular physique that was accentuated by his form fitting black t-shirt. His hair was cut low and his waves spun in a 360-degree circular motion. He wore a perfectly shaped up goatee that showed his age with the salt and pepper sprinkled evenly throughout the hairs on his chin. His eyes were green and he wore a soft yellow Stacy Adams linen suit with black Gator shoes. He smiled revealing his white perfectly shaped and evenly spaced teeth. His cologne smelled heavenly and it was something I never smelled before. He removed an unlit cigar from his mouth.

"Mmm mmm mmm, I'm glad you're looking for me."

I noticed how he was looking at me and it made me uncomfortable so I decided to quickly put an end to the stare.

"Are you Jimmy?" I asked, nervously.

"Well if I ain't, my momma lied to me years ago." he joked extending his hand for a handshake. His hand was full of jewelry, a diamond pinky ring and a watch that had so many diamonds in the face that I could fix my hair in it.

A Gangster's Melody

I extended my hand as well "Hello sir. I'm Tiffany. I'm Lula Belle's granddaughter." We shook hands.

"Oh okay baby. I have been expecting you. Follow me." He led me through the restaurant that was even more elegant inside than outside.

The décor was incredibly tasteful. It was all black and gold themed. The walls were covered in black art. And the ceilings held chandeliers that looked like they cost a million dollars each. I noticed that the cooks, Maitre De', and manager were black but all of the servers and bus boys were white. I guess Mr. Jimmy was on some black power trip, but that didn't bother me. It was actually kind of interesting to see the roles reversed for a change.

When we got to his office he opened two very large doors that led into an office that was about as big as some studio apartments I had been in. There was a 50 inch plasma T.V. on the wall. The desk was made of cherry wood. There was also a large black leather sofa. Directly underneath the plasma television was a fireplace. He instructed me to take a seat in a large black leather chair as he took his seat on the other side of the desk. He crossed his hands and placed them on the desk and leaned forward.

"So you're Lula Belle's grandbaby huh?"

"Yes sir I am"

"Please call me Jimmy, sir sounds so old."

"Yes sir. I mean Jimmy." He laughed, briefly and started the interview.

"So Tiffany, do you have any experience?"

"Unfortunately, Mr. Jimmy I don't."

"Well that's ok. The job is easy. Just take the orders and bring them back to the kitchen. When the chef announces that your order is ready you go to the window and check the order to make sure it's right. If it's right then you alert one of the servers. Under NO circumstances are you to serve the food yourself. I'm sure from the little tour I gave you; you can see how I run things around here."

I smiled. "Sounds simple enough," I said.

"It is. That's why I'm going to start you at 6 dollars an hour. But don't worry, this place is popular so if you play your cards right you can make a couple hundred a week just in tips. So when can you start?"

I was shocked by the automatic hire.

"Wow when do you want me to start?" He smiled, obviously happy that I accepted his offer.

"Well it will be kind of slow this morning but you can start now if you want. I'll get you an apron and start you at a slow station." He left to get me an apron and I was actually happy for the first time in the past 24 hours.

If this job went the way I thought it would I would be able to save up enough money to move out on my own in a few months. I thought of all the nice things I would buy myself. I also thought of going to get my cosmetology license and eventually opening my own salon one day. I only wished mama and daddy were alive to see me achieve my dreams.

Mr. Jimmy coming back into the room snapped me out of my daydream.

"Here you go sweetie," He said, handing me an apron, pad and a pen to take the orders with. He pointed to the video monitors on his desk that showed surveillance of the whole restaurant. He pointed at a table.

"Okay baby. That's table 7 right over there where those girls are sitting, that's yours for the next few days until you get your feet wet. Don't be nervous, you'll be fine."

But no matter how much he assured me, I was nervous like the first black President on inauguration

A Gangster's Melody 21

day. I slowly got up, put on my apron, gathered my nerves and headed back into the main dining area. I silently gave myself a mental pep talk as I got closer and closer to the table.

"You can do this, you can do this." I kept saying to myself. When I got to the table the three girls at the table were engulfed in a conversation. I held my head high mustered up all my courage and interrupted.

"Good morning ladies. How may I help you?" They looked up, noticed me and just kept talking like I wasn't even there. I waited a few seconds and offered my help again.

"Excuse me ladies, how can I help you this morning?" The girl closest to the window responded first.

"Calm down bitch we heard you. Can't you see we fuckin talking?" I was taken aback by her rudeness.

"Miss, the vulgarity and name calling is not called for."

The girl next to her sprung into action and pulled a stra'ight razor from her bra.

"What you gonna do about it bitch?" At this point I was scared to death, so I played it smart so these girls wouldn't jump on me and possibly slit my throat.

"Look ladies, I'm sorry. I didn't want to start nothing. I just wanted to take your orders, but I can come back when you finish talking." I turned to leave and the third girl spoke up next.

"Hold on little mama. We ready to order. Ya'll chill the fuck out. Ya'll see she's new around here. Ain't you little mama?" she said, smiling at me almost as if she were flirting. But I responded to her because she was obviously the friendly one and god forbid something jumped off, she seemed like she could control the other two.

"As a matter of fact, I am new here. I just got here last night." I now found myself engulfed in a conversation with girl #3.

She responded to the information I gave her. "Okay. That's what's up, where you from?" I had become a little more relaxed now.

"I'm from Marion, Ohio." I responded.

"Damn shawty, what brings you here?"

"Trust me, it's a long story."

She started fishing for answers. "Well let's see, you way too square to be running from the law. You chasing a nigga?"

"No." I said adamantly.

"Oh shit. You running from one?"

"No." I said more adamantly than the first time.

"Then why you here?"

Okay that was it. She had worked my last nerve. "Look I don't wanna talk about it so are ya'll gonna order or what?" I said, my voice now showing how agitated I was. The girl who had pulled the razor spoke her mind next.

"Yo fuck this bitch Monica."

"Nah. Fuck ya'll. Ya'll bitches can starve." I responded. And with that said I turned on my heels and stormed off. I snatched off my apron as I headed back to Mr. Jimmy's office to tell him what had happened, but to my surprise he was standing at the kitchen door watching the whole thing. As I approached he looked at his watch and shook his head.

"Wow. Four minutes and quitting already? That's got to be a new record."

"Mr. Jimmy I'm sorry, but maybe this ain't the job for me. Those bitches, excuse my language, those girls were rude and very disrespectful. One of them even pulled a razor on me. And I should not, and will not go through that at work." My eyes started tearing up as I

A Gangster's Melody   23

fought to control my emotions. Mr. Jimmy put his arm around me.

"Look, Tiffany, I know your background and I know why you are here in Baltimore. I also watched that whole situation go down with that crew of girls over there. So I know what set you off. And that is my fault. I should have warned you that in this business you are going to run into some assholes, both men and women. Now it's obvious to me that they struck a very sensitive nerve with you, so I'll tell you what, you run on home and think on it, and if you still want the job then come back tomorrow at 3pm and we'll start all over again."

"Ok. Mr. Jimmy, I'll do that. And once again I'm sorry."

"No need to apologize sweety."

I took my cell phone off my hip and proceeded to dial Mama Belle's number until the recording alerted me that I was out of pre-paid minutes.

"You gotta be kidding me." I said out loud to no one in particular.

"What's wrong Tiffany?" Mr. Jimmy said noticing that I was upset.

"My cell phone is out of minutes and I'm trying to call my Grandmother to come and pick me up."

"Well if you like, you can use the phone in my office."

"Thank you Mr. Jimmy. This won't take long.

Once I was back in his office I sat in the big leather chair on his side of the desk, picked up the phone and once again dialed Mama Belle's number. After the phone rang about eight times the answering machine picked up playing some old gospel record. I hung up and dialed her cell phone number only to get the exact same response with the exact same song on the answering machine. Mr. Jimmy must have noticed the frustration on my face.

"Is there a problem baby?" he asked politely.

"Ain't nobody answering the phone." I responded trying not to sound too annoyed.

"She probably just stepped out for a minute, but it's a beautiful day outside Tiffany and you only live a few blocks from here. It would probably only take you ten or fifteen minutes to walk home. All you have to do is take Fayette to Prince and make a left.

"Sounds like I don't have a choice, maybe she will be there by the time I get home. Well, I better get going. If she calls or comes by just tell her I decided to walk okay Mr. Jimmy?

"Sure thing sweety. And I hope to see you tomorrow."

"Well I will definitely give it some thought, but no matter what I decide I will call you." And with that being said I grabbed my purse and left.

LOVE THY NEIGHBOR

Mr. Jimmy was right. It was a beautiful day outside so I didn't mind the walk. I still couldn't get over how congested the streets of Baltimore were. As I walked home I was repeatedly holla'd at by guys that were passing by, either walking or driving. Some of them drove cars that I only saw in music videos. And while I may have been a little excited about all of the attention I was getting, I ignored the gestures, all of the "HEY SHAWTY'S" , and the horn blowing. My daddy had told me ever since I was a little girl that the day would come when men would only want to get in my pants. He also told me that while most men were full of shit that I should be extra conscious of big city guys with their fancy cars and slick talking asses. So with that in mind I just smiled to myself and continued to walk home. When I reached the house I saw that Mama Belle's car was nowhere in sight but I decided to ring the bell anyway just for shits and giggles. And just like I thought, there was no answer. There was nothing else I could do but sit on the porch and wait, hoping that she wouldn't be gone too long because it was hot as hell. To occupy my time I decided to do the crossword puzzle that I had brought with me for the long bus ride. So I sat on the porch, pulled a pen and the crossword book out of my purse and got busy trying to figure out the hard puzzles. I must have been doing the puzzles for about ten or fifteen minutes when I heard the sound of high-heeled shoes click clacking up the sidewalk. I was too engulfed into figuring out a fifteen-letter word for a zoo animal to look up to see who the shoes were attached to. The click clacking stopped right in front of me. I noticed the expensive stilettos and the well pedicured feet with the diamond tennis bracelet around the ankle, the rest of the body spoke before I looked up.

"Well, well, well, Lil mama, what you doing sitting on Ms. Lula-Belle's porch?

It was Monica from the diner. I immediately jumped up.

"Hey. Did you follow me home?" Okay. Let's go then."

I then got into what I thought was a very good fighting stance, but the truth of the matter is I had never actually been in a real fight before and I guess it was evident because Monica took one look at me and burst out laughing.

"Hold on shawty. Calm down shit. Ain't nobody here to fuck with you. I live next door and I wanted to know what you was doing sitting on my neighbors porch is all."

"So what's so damn funny then?" I asked still holding my ridiculous fighting stance.

"Cuz you tryna sound all gangster, and that shit ain't believable at all. But it's all good though. At least you ain't no punk bitch."

We both shared a slight laugh.

"Anyway shawty, my name is Monica." She said extending her hand. I reluctantly dropped my guard and returned the gesture.

"Hi, my name is Tiffany."

"Oh. Okay. Well anyway, what you doing on Ms. Lula-Belle's porch? If she catch you hanging out here she gonna either scream on you, throw hot water out the window, or both. She a cool old lady but she can be a real bitch sometimes."

"I know. She's my grandmother." I responded sort of embarrassed.

A Gangster's Melody 27

"Oh my bad Tiffany. I ain't no Ms. Lula-Belle was ya folks."

"It's all good. Believe me. I know how she can be."

"Well I been living here for years and I ain't never knew Ms. Lula–Belle even had a granddaughter." I was hit with the sudden urge to tell my story.

"Well it's like this." She waived her hand and cut me off.

"Hold on Tiff. This sounds like it's gonna be a long ass story and I gotta take my medicine. So let's go next door to my crib so we can chill and you can fill me in."

"Okay cool. Let's go. It's getting hot as hell out here anyway."

"I know that's right, that's why I left the air conditioner in my crib running all morning."

We went next door to her house and although it was only right next door it looked way more expensive than Mama Belle's house. The outside was light blue with white trimming and it looked like it had just been freshly pain'ted. The grass was freshly cut and a beautiful shade of green. When we got into the house it was decorated in expensive décor. There was black art and gold light fixtures along the walls leading up the staircase. When we got upstairs I was instructed to remove my shoes. And I immediately understood why. Her carpet was as white as brand new cotton socks, and when you stepped on it, you felt as if you sank all the way down to your knees. Her furniture looked expensive as well. In the living room there was a black and white leather sectional and a matching love seat. On the wall was a 56 inch plasma television and there were framed pictures of her and the girls I saw her with earlier. There were also pictures of guys holding wads of money and throwing it money up in the air. She noticed me looking around and broke the silence.

"So you like what you see?"

28   *Sean Wright*

"Hell yeah. This crib is hot as hell. Ya moms and pops must make good money."

"Moms and pops? Shit girl, my moms live across town in a inpatient rehab center and the last I heard about that cum distributor they call my pops, he was in jail somewhere."

"Well who lives here with you then?" I asked, still in shock from the way she spoke about her parents.

"Not a fucking soul. This is my shit. I live alone and everything in this bitch is mine. Ain't no fuckin rent to own either." She said proudly.

"Well shit girl, how old are you and what kind of job you got that gets you all of this?" I asked curiously.

"I'm 19 and my boss pays very well as you can see. You wanna meet her?"

"Hell yeah where is she?" I asked all excited.

And without warning Monica grabbed my hand and put it up her skirt.

"Here she is right here. The best boss a bitch can ever have. The pay is excellent and the hours are flexible."

I pulled my hand back in a total state of shock.

"Girl are you a prostitute?"

Monica just let out a slight chuckle. "Well not in that sense of the word, but shit, niggas that I fuck with know that they gotta pay to play. My mortgage, lights, gas, wardrobe, everything is paid for. All the way down to my mother's commissary. And I keep money in the bank to stay on top of the name game ya dig?"

"The name game?" I asked just as dumbfounded.

"Yeah. You know, Ed Hardy, Juicy Couture? Shit like that."

I was still lost and it must have shown that I was a little taken back by the thought of this young girl in front of me doing sexual favors for money and material things. Monica interrupted my train of thought.

A Gangster's Melody 29

"Don't give me that look. You ain't never let a nigga drill you down before or after taking you shopping or buying you something? It's the same shit."

"Girl hell no. Nigga's where I'm from ain't no ballers."

"So back home you was breaking nigga's off for free? Bitch you crazy." Monica said sounding a little aggravated. My eyes dropped to the carpet as I answered.

"Well...to be honest with you." She cut me off.

"Oh hell naw. Girl is you a virgin? How old are you?"

"Nineteen." I responded bashfully. Monica burst out laughing.

"Damn. They still make ya'll? I got to meet ya moms and pops."

She had instantly struck a nerve.

"Look they're dead okay. They died together in a car accident." I said lying and showing more emotion than I wanted to.

"Oh shit girl. I'm sorry." Monica said sounding remorseful.

"It's okay. You didn't know. But it's still fresh so can we change the subject?"

"Oh fa sho. I don't wanna upset you. So what do you wanna talk about?"

"Hmm. Let's finish talking about yo hoe ass." We both laughed before Monica continued.

"Okay. I'm gonna school you. But first I need to take my medicine."

I followed her into the kitchen and I watched as she dug her hand into a box of cereal. She pulled out a zip lock bag full of weed. There was a blunt already rolled. She took it out and closed the bag. Then she stuffed it back in the box. She shook the box and put it back in the cabinet. Then she put the blunt in her mouth and lit it.

"I thought you said you had to take ya medicine." Once again I was lost and confused. Monica inhaled deeply and answered my question.

"Shit. You ain't know? This *is* my medicine. Now sit down and let me school you.

We sat on the couch facing each other and then Monica continued.

"Okay first things first. I'm gonna take you under my wing. You gonna be my special project, but you ain't in the suburbs of Bumfuck , Ohio no more. You in B-more, the belly of the fucking beast where you gotta grind to survive. See, pretty bitches like me, you and them two knuckle heads I was with earlier will have niggas eating out the palm of our hands. I'm gonna show you the ropes if you willing to learn. Cuz I know you ain't tryna stay with Miss Lula Belle too long."

"Hell naw. I'm tryna roll with you." I answered excitedly.

She passed me the blunt and I took a pull pretending again to know what I was doing and damn near choked to death.

"You gotta slow down ma. That's that Sour Diesel. You gotta walk that dog slow." Monica instructed. I was still choking when I answered her.

"I ain't never smoked before."

"Aww damn. We got a lot of work to do. Okay if you gonna be one of my Stiletto Diva's then ya gear gotta be up to par. So I'm gonna have Terri boost you some really hot shit. Then I'm gonna get Lashawn to tighten ya wig up. And tomorrow you gonna roll with us to Dreamscape." I was already high as hell.

"Dream what?" I asked slurring my words with my eyes half closed.

A Gangster's Melody 31

"Dreamscape. That's where all the big ballers party at. Now there ain't a baller in Baltimore that I don't know, so I'm gonna find you a good one. One that I know is gonna trick on you and before you know it you gonna have all of this just like me."

"Shit. That's what's up." I said. Now even more excited.

"Oh yeah. One more thing. The only thing I love as much as weed, dick and money is pussy. So watch ya'self pretty. Cuz I'm coming for you...literally." She said smiling and licking her lips

"So you gay? I don't get down like that." I stated matter of factly."

"First of all sexy, none of the Stiletto Diva's are gay. We just enjoy a little pussy from time to time. And don't worry ain't nobody gonna rape you. Sooner or later you'll give it to me." She said licking her lips again. Monica then reached under the cushion in her couch and pulled out a very large sex toy.

"Well, that concludes today's lesson. Now run on home. I've got some business to tend to. And unless you gonna play with me I'm gonna need you to lock the door on ya way out. If anything goes down tonight I'll holla at you."

I just shook my head in amazement. "Okay girl. Get at me later."

Monica grabbed the remote control and turned on a porno movie that was already queued up in the DVD player. As I headed down the stairs I could hear her starting the festivities, she was moaning and groaning. I closed the door and shook my head smiling. I turned around to see Mama Belle standing in front of the house.

"There you go. What in the hell are you doing coming out of that house? She barked at me.

"I was locked out so my friend Monica let me chill over her house for a little while."

"Girl get your ass in the house. You ain't here a full twenty four hours yet and you hanging with dykes already?"

I rolled my eyes and walked passed Mama Belle and she immediately smelled the weed on me.

"And you been smoking that shit too? You gonna fuck around and find ya'self homeless a lot sooner than later."

I had forgotten all about the weed smell. How could I have not remembered that? I just kept walking to the house and once we got inside she didn't let up one bit.

"You know you starting off on the wrong damn foot already. You walked out on your job, you dress all trampish, and then you next door getting high and doing god knows what with that damn lesbian. Are you a lesbian Tiffany? You like the pretty ladies? Cuz if you do you can just carry all that sinful foolishness away from here. This here is a god fearing household."

"Look grandma. Number one, I didn't walk out on the job. I was given permission to leave. Number two, okay, I smoked a little weed with Monica but guess what grandma? I'm a grown and very responsible woman. I am no longer the little girl you saw years ago. And as far as me being a lesbian, not only am I offended but I'm hurt that my own grandmother could say something so disrespectful to me, especially since I haven't even been with a man yet. Oh don't look surprised. Yes Mama Belle I'm still a virgin. And last but not least. As far as my clothes go. I would ask my parents to take me shopping, but in case you didn't get the memo they are both FUCKING DEAD."

I had totally spazzed out on Mama Belle then I stormed out of the house and left her standing there in total amazement. When I got outside I just sat on the

A Gangster's Melody 33

porch and began to cry uncontrollably. I stopped momentarily when I saw two cars pull up. One was a brand new Mercedes, and the other appeared to be a convertible BMW but I really couldn't tell. All I know was that they were both expensive and brand new. Monica had come out of the house and greeted the driver of the Mercedes with a hug and a kiss. Then he gave her the keys and got in the BMW with the other guy and they left. Monica got in the Mercedes and was about to pull off, but when she noticed me on the porch she stopped in front of my house.

"What up girl? You trying to ride out with me?"

"Hell yeah. Anything to get away from here." I said jumping up and wiping my tears. I hurried over to the car and got in and we pulled off.

"So where we goin?" I asked anxiously.

"That depends. Open up the glove compartment. How much money is in there?"

I took the wad of money out and counted it silently.

"$2,500" I responded in amazement.

"Damn that nigga getting cheap. Okay first stop is the nail salon, my treat.

"Look girl, I appreciate it and everything but I don't have any money right now so I don't know when I will be able to pay you back."

"Bitch please. Ain't nobody trippin off no bread, you can't take that shit with you. Besides, by the time I'm finished spending this $2500, some other pussy whipped nigga will throw some more bread my way. It just goes in one big beautiful circle."

"Damn it's like that out here?"

"Nah baby. It's like that everywhere. Niggas work for the pussy, so you gotta make the pussy work for you. But don't worry; I'm going to show you how to never be broke again. That is, if you are willing to learn."

"Hell yeah. Teach on girl." I laughed as we weaved in and out of traffic.

A NEW BALLER IN TOWN

TRAVON

I was in my hotel suite sitting on the edge of the bed when my cell phone rang, it was my boy Sincere.

"Hello? What's good my nigga? Oh yeah. I been in town for about two hours now. Well I had to stop by the mall and pick up a few things. You know I gotta come to the club fresh to death. What did I get? Nothing really. A couple of outfits with matching kicks, some socks, boxers and a bad bitch, you know the usual. Well you know how I do. Yeah I'll meet you at the club around twelve. Be out front where I can find you. Yeah that's what's up. Yeah D-boy and L.V. should be here any minute now to pick up that package. A'ight, well look. I'll hit you back in a few. Right now I'm trying out something that I got at the mall. A'ight my nigga I'll holla."

I hung up the phone and focused my attention on the best thing that I brought back from the mall.

"Okay ma stop. There's no way I should have been able to finish that call if you was really good with ya head game. So obviously that ain't ya specialty."

"Damn daddy you ain't gotta be all rude with it. Ya'll New York niggas is something else."

"I ain't being rude ma. I'm being real but it's all good. No hard feelings."

"Uh Uh. I ain't goin out like that"

The next thing I knew she had pushed me back on the bed and raised her sundress over her head and took it off showing that she wore no bra and no underwear.

"Now let me show you how real B-More bitches get down."

Without hesitation she mounted me and rode me like a true rodeo champ. I'll keep it real. I had been all over and I can only remember a hand full of chicks that knew how to work the pussy like shorty. To be honest I'm glad she knew how to fuck, because her head game was wack as fuck. As she gyrated her hips on my dick I did the same and met each downward thrust with an upward thrust of my own. She dug her nails into my chest as I continuously hit her G-spot. With each stroke she bit her bottom lip and told me how much she liked the sex. She didn't scream my name because I don't think she remembered it. I wasn't mad though. I didn't remember her name either. All I remember is she was a bad bitch that was buying her man some sneakers because he was locked up. And now here she was, getting fucked all crazy by a smooth nigga she just met. If her man only knew.

Shortly after I fucked her to sleep there was a knock at the door. I instinctively grabbed my Desert Eagle from underneath the pillow and headed for the door. I looked out the peephole and saw it was my people D-Boy and L.V. They were the two main members of the famous rap group the Realm Squad. I managed them and they also doubled as my ride or die cats in these streets. I mean, yeah we was getting a little money with the music shit but please don't believe the videos and MTV cribs. A lot of niggas in the rap game still hustle because they got to eat. And like I said before, the music industry don't really pay shit. So we use the music industry as a front and continue to do what we do best, selling coke. I opened the door and greeted them both with daps and hugs.

"What's good fam?" I asked as if I didn't already know the answer.

A Gangster's Melody   37

"Damn baby, was we interrupting?" D-Boy asked noticing the jump off sprawled across the bed totally naked and fast asleep.

"Shit, evidently not. It looks like he's finished to me." L.V. responded. We all shared a laugh that woke the girl from her sleep. Before she could focus her eyes on the two rising stars in front of her she grabbed the covers and assumed the worst.

"Uh Uh. What the fuck ya'll trying to do? Ain't no freak shit jumping off in here." she screamed in anger.

"Whoa. Slow down baby, ain't nothing happening. These are my friends and they just came to get something and then they leaving." I quickly responded trying to calm her down.

"I don't give a fuck who…hold on. Ain't ya'll them Realm Squad niggas? Oh shit. You ain't tell me you knew them." She said, now not caring and letting the covers fall to the floor exposing her naked body.

"Well look ma. They headed towards your neck of the woods. So why don't you let them drop you off? Ya'll don't mind do you?" I asked winking my eye at D-boy.

"Nah baby we don't mind at all. We just have to stop by our hotel first. Is that cool with you?" D-Boy said, setting the bait and reeling her in.

"Hell yeah. It's all good. I ain't in no rush. We can kick it for a while." She said taking the bait. She then grabbed her clothes and headed to the bathroom.

"Okay fellas. While we wait for her to get dressed let's get down to business." I suggested. Then I pulled a duffle bag from under the bed and handed it to D-boy.

"Make sure that gets where it needs to go." I instructed.

"Don't worry kid, we got this." L.V. responded.

The girl had come out of the bathroom smiling and looking just as good as when I brought her back to the hotel.

"You ready to go sexy?" D-boy asked, looking her up and down.

"Yeah let's go." She said, licking her lips and smiling.

"Yo. We'll catch up with you later at the club." L.V. said, then they both gave me dap and left.

I closed and locked the door behind them. Then I emptied the bags of clothes that I had got from the mall out on the bed and tried to decide which outfit to wear later that night. After deciding black jeans, black fitted shirt and the new Gucci shoes I bought, I picked up the phone to call Sincere back.

"Yeah what's good? Everything's a go for tonight, D-boy and L.V. just left with the package. So like I said, be at the club around twelve, and bring some of them dime ass chicks you know and put them on the V.I.P. list. I got a strange feeling I'm going to want some company after the club….a'ight nigga peace."

PARTY TIME

Monica and I were leaving the mall both of us with a hand full of bags headed to the car, when Monica got a call on her cell phone. I wasn't sure who it was but I heard something about a party and V.I.P. treatment. And who ever she was talking to she was sure to point out the fact that the Stiletto Divas would be there and that we weren't going to pay for anything all night. She finally hung up the phone and turned to me, by this time I was hanging on to every word.

"Well, what's going on?" I asked, all exited.

"That was my boy Sincere. He said the Realm Squad is in town and they got a party going on tonight. And he wants us to hold the down V.I.P. section." She answered.

"Oh for real? That's what's up. I like they new song. They really want us to hold down the V.I.P?" I asked. I couldn't believe what I was hearing.

"Hell yeah. They already know how the SD's get down. That's why they call us whenever there is a baller event going on. So it's a good thing we did some shopping and got our hair and nails done. So pay attention because tonight will be lesson number one on how to bag a baller." She advised me. Then it hit me like a ton of bricks.

"The only problem is my Grandmother. If I stay out all night she is going to flip out." I said, now sounding depressed.

"Well I can't help you with that, and I damn sure ain't cutting my night short to bring you home so you better handle your business."

We put the bags in the trunk and got in the car. I slumped down in the passenger's seat no longer excited, and no longer in such a good mood. How was I

40   *Sean Wright*

going to get around arguing with Mama Belle about going out tonight? It was times like this I really missed mommy and daddy. Monica was on her cell phone alerting the rest of the crew when we pulled up in front of my house. She finished up her call and turned to me.

"Look I'll be back to get you at 10:30. If you ain't going then call my cell phone." She instructed.

"Okay girl, let me go in and deal with the bullshit. I'll holla at you. Where you going anyway?" I asked curiously.

"Shit. We spent a lot of money today. I'm going to get some more and switch up whips." She stated as if it was a part of her everyday routine.

"Girl you are something else. Thanks for the shopping spree." I said very appreciative.

"It ain't shit. You can repay me by just being a down ass loyal bitch. Anyway I'll holla." She drove off and I watched her head get smaller going down the block.

When I got inside the house I headed stra'ight for my room. Once inside my room I emptied out all of the bags from the mall onto that little ass bed. I had so much stuff that the bed couldn't hold them all. I picked up the Juicy Couture outfit held it under my chin, and thought to myself *"I'm going to kill them in this, especially with the matching shoes and belt."* I was just in the middle of making myself feel good again when Mama Belle walked in. She noticed the makeover and all the clothes and immediately started preaching.

"You know child, I came in here to have a talk with you woman to woman, but now I see all these fancy clothes, the hairdo and the nails, and I know you ain't got no damn money. You wanna explain this shit?" She asked with a sarcastic attitude.

"Grandma, Monica bought me all of this so I would look nice when we went out tonight. She knew I didn't

A Gangster's Melody   41

have anything so she treated me. And I happen to think it was very nice of her." I stated matter of factly.

"You know you're about as dumb as a bag of bricks if you think that a total stranger is going to spend a bunch of money on you for no reason. There ain't that much niceness in the world. That damn lesbian ain't nothing but trouble. Jumping in and out of all those fancy cars. Her and all her fast ass friends. And if you think you gonna run the streets all times of night and come in here when you feel like it you got another thing coming." She said, shaking one finger in my face with her other hand on her hip

"Look grandma, I'm just going out for a few hours with Monica and a few of her friends. I can take care of myself and I know right from wrong. You are just going to have to trust me." I responded.

"Trust you? You know right from wrong? Girl this is Baltimore, Maryland. These fast ass streets will eat your little country ass up and spit you out. But okay, Miss know it all, you go on ahead. You been here 24 hours and you think you got Baltimore all figured out huh? Well I'm going to sit back and watch the show but don't say I didn't warn you." She said, with a sinister smile on her face. Then she closed the door and left.

I closed my eyes and plopped down on my bed. I looked at the clock and realized it was 8:30 and decided I better get myself ready. I grabbed my washcloth, underwear and robe and headed to take a shower. While in the shower all I could think about was how much fun I would have later on that night. I also made a mental note to be responsible and come home at a decent hour. Even if it meant leaving the girls and taking a cab home. Monica had given me some spending money to put in my pocket. Although she swore up and down that as long as I was with her I wouldn't need to spend it. I was very appreciative, but

I hated being dependant on people but what other choice did I have? Daddy's life insurance policy was null and void since it was a suicide, neither he or momma had a will and the money they had saved up paid for the double funeral. So I was left with absolutely nothing. And although I hated taking handouts, at this point I had to do what I had to do.

I was dressed and on my way out the door when I was stopped by Mama Belle. She handed me some house keys.

"Here, this is so you don't wake me up when you get back here. And even though I'm giving you a key, you better bring your ass back here at a decent hour."

"And what's a decent hour Grandma?" I asked, fearing the worst.

"You're grown remember? Figure it out." She responded sarcastically.

With that being said, she turned and left me standing right there, I hurried up and left before she returned with more of her ranting. When I got outside Monica was waiting in a brand new candy apple red Range Rover with Big black rims.

"Girl hurry up, we got a tight schedule to keep." She yelled, out of the window.

"I'm coming, I'm coming." I answered back, rushing to the car.

"Damn girl, You are wearing the hell out of that outfit." She said, complimenting me on my attire.

"Thanks Monica, but I owe it all to you. I'd still be in those country rags if it wasn't for you." I stated, very appreciative.

"I told you girl. It ain't nothing but dough, you can't take this shit with you. And besides it ain't mines anyway." We both shared a laugh.

Friday night's in Baltimore was like nothing I had ever seen before. The streets were alive and buzzing

A Gangster's Melody 43

with an energy that was out of this world. As we drove to the club we pulled up alongside a lot of fancy and expensive cars that played loud music and had passengers that appeared to be just as expensive and fancy as the cars they were in. I was shocked and amazed yet again as we cruised through the streets of Baltimore. As we went from block to block, each one looked as if it hosted its own after party. There were people everywhere. Monica must have noticed the tourist look on my face.

"You're a long way from Kansas ain't you Dorothy?" she said, jokingly.

"Yeah girl, this shit is crazy. I think I'm going to love Baltimore."

"Uh Uh. That's where you are wrong. Rule #1 don't love nobody or nothing but yourself. Follow that rule and you will make it a lot further in life." She stated, firmly. Almost as if she was scolding me.

"Okay. I got you." I said just agreeing with her but not really understanding how you could go through life not loving anything or anyone.

When we pulled into the club parking lot it, it was like I was at one of those car shows I would see on the news or on the internet. There were ballers everywhere. And I had never seen so much jewelry in my life. If I had to take a guess I would say there was well over a million dollars worth of jewelry just in the parking lot alone. And I'm not just talking about the men. I ain't no hater, the women were all dressed to impress. And even they were flooded with platinum and diamonds. And even they were driving exotic cars. Some of them were even riding motorcycles. There was a crew of female riders whose motorcycles were all pink and they had on pink leather riding outfits. They looked really nice. They were in the parking lot doing tricks and everything. I was hooked and didn't even know it.

"Damn it's poppin' out here." I said, sounding like a true tourist.

"Girl this ain't shit, it's still early. Give it about another hour and motherfuckers will be asshole to elbow. Here spark this so we can get our mind right before we go in." She said, handing me a blunt before continuing.

"Now once we get inside, you just follow my lead and I'll point out all the prospects. I'll show you all of the money makers and all the fucking fakers." She instructed, as I passed the blunt back.

"So how do you know who's who?" I asked, ready to learn.

"Well that's easy for me, because I know almost everybody in B-More. So I know all the major players in town. Now we have to have a few ground rules to go over. #1- Stick by my side all night. The Stiletto Divas always stick together because we got some bitches hating on us. #2- Don't give no nigga the time of day without checking with one of us first. Reason being, it might be somebody man, baby daddy, or just a plain old no good nigga. And last but not least, you don't leave with no nigga. We come together, we leave together. If you want to hook up with a nigga you have him meet you later." She instructed.

"Okay. I feel you....Damn. I'm high as fuck." I slurred with my eyes half closed.

"Well don't get in there and act all crazy and shit. Just chill and do the weed, don't let the weed do you." She said.

After a brief moment of silence Monica's cell phone rang.

"Yeah what's up?...yeah me and my girl Tiffany is in the parking lot right now getting blowed. Nah. You

A Gangster's Melody   45

don't know her. She's a new edition to the click. She only been in town a day and already she running with the baddest bitch. Yeah she stra'ight from Ohio. Hold on Sincere, that's Terri and them on the other line. As a matter of fact I'll hit you when we get to the door. Hello? Yeah Terri what's up? Yeah we in the back by the gate. I got Pooda's truck. Alright bring the L's and whatever ya'll got to drink." She hung up the phone and pulled down the mirror to fix her makeup.

"Yo. I'm excited as shit. I ain't never really been to a club before." I said, breaking the silence.

"Well look. Don't go in there acting like no tourist or no groupie because best believe if you act like a nut I will leave your country ass right here." She responded jokingly, but I sensed that she might have meant it.

Within minutes Terri and Lashawn pulled up and got in the car with us.

"What's up bitches?" Terri asked. She was the one who pulled the blade on me in the diner.

"Ya'll bitches get in and shut the door, you letting the smoke out." Monica demanded.

"Aww bitch, shut up. We got plenty of weed and something to wash it down with." Lashawn responded, holding up a bottle of some sort of liquor. I think they were calling it *Patron*.

"Well hurry up and put that shit in rotation before it's time to go in." Monica said, looking in the rear view window.

"Ya'll remember Tiffany right?" she continued.

"How can I forget little miss waitress? I almost had to cut her ass." Terri said, looking at me and rolling her eyes. I was feeling the effects of the weed so the timid and shy Tiffany from earlier went right out the window.

"Yeah, well try that shit again and you will eat that fucking razor." I snapped back at her.

"What?" She responded in astonishment.

"Hey ya'll bitches fall the fuck back. Now Tiffany is cool and she is going to be one of the girls from now on, so ya'll squash that bullshit. Now ya'll take ya last pulls and ya last shots and let's head inside." Monica jumped in.

As if Monica was the General leading this army of bad bitches, we all followed her instructions and piled out of the car. As we headed towards the front of the club dudes tried to holler at us and chicks gave us the evil eye. But one thing is for sure *EVERYONE* knew the Stiletto Divas whether they loved them or hated them. When we got to the front of the club I noticed that the line seemed to be never ending. Men were claiming that they knew the owner and women were complaining about their feet hurting from standing on line so long. But following Monica's lead we went stra'ight to the front of the line. We just kept going and paid no attention to the haters as the bouncers unhooked the red velvet rope and ushered us inside. Once we were inside Monica's friend Sincere came to the lobby to meet us. Sincere was tall and slim. About 6 foot 2 and fair skinned. He was dressed nice and had an aura about him that just said money.

"What's up ladies? Damn. Ya'll are looking good tonight." He said, giving us the once over.

"Don't we always baby?" LaShawn answered, stroking his chin.

"Girl, don't start nothing you can't finish." He responded flirtatiously.

"Nigga you already know. Get your paper right and get back at me." LaShawn fired back.

"It ain't about the money baby girl, it's about being labeled as a trick. And you know my stats are way too high for that. Now ya'll come on." Sincere responded, ending the verbal cat and mouse game.

A Gangster's Melody 47

We followed Sincere through the club and headed to the V.I.P. section. In between the front door and the V.I.P. section Monica, Terri, and LaShawn each stopped briefly to talk to men and women that they knew. When we finally made our way through the crowd and got to the V.I.P area two very large bodyguards stepped to the side and allowed our entrance. Once inside I could see that it was packed with wall to wall ballers popping *Kristal,* taking pills, and smoking weed. There were females hovering over any man they could get a hold of. Sincere led us over to a very private section of the V.I.P.

"Ya'll ladies make yourselves comfortable. We're going to get this party started in a few." He instructed as he walked off.

"C'mon ya'll let's take this table over here where we can get a good view of whose coming and going." Monica said, directing us to a table with a good view.

"Damn. There are some good looking guys in here. I ain't never seen so many ballers in my life." I said, sounding like a kid in a candy store.

"Girl please, we damn near know every guy in this room and all of them ain't no damn ballers. I can personally point out a few fakers right now. For example, see the high yellow nigga over there in the white Armani linen suit with the platinum chain and platinum grill going a little too hard at that ghetto bird?" LaShawn asked.

"Hell yeah. That dude looks good as hell." I responded a little over excited.

"That's Leroy. He's a faker. The Armani suit is boot legged, that's white gold around his neck the diamonds are Cubic Zirconium, his grill is silver and that bitch is too low class to know the difference." She said, schooling me.

"Damn. He had me fooled." I said, feeling stupid.

"Yeah. But you don't know no better. Now that guy over there in the blue...faker..in the green..faker..I could go on forever pointing out the scrubs in here." LaShawn stated, still giving me my lesson.

"Well who is that over there?" I asked, pointing to the guy who just walked in.

"Shit. I don't know. I ain't never seen him before but I'm damn sure going to find out." LaShawn answered, sounding just as eager as I was to find out who he was.

The guy was averaged sized. About 5'8 or 5'9 with a smooth caramel complexion. His hair was cut low and his waves were making me sea sick. He also had a goatee that was well groomed. His physical stature was that of an NFL running back. He was stocky and the tight fit black muscle shirt that he wore accentuated every cut of muscle that he possessed. He also wore black designer jeans and a pair of black Gucci shoes. In his ear there was a diamond earring that reflected off his watch and small diamond encrusted pendant that hung from the Platinum necklace that hung from his neck. Whoever this man was, all eyes were definitely on him.

"Hey, ya'll see that?" LaShawn asked, talking to Terri and Monica.

"Yeah we see." They both responded in unison.

"I don't know who the hell he is, but I smell money. And lot's of it." Monica said, not taking her eyes off of the mystery man.

Just then the music cut off and the lights got low. The D.J. was ready to make an announcement.

"Okay. Now for the moment you have all been waiting for. Get up and put your hands together for The Realm Squad." The D.J. announced.

A Gangster's Melody   49

The crowd was going crazy as the hottest rap group out hit the stage. I still couldn't believe I was watching the whole thing from the V.I.P. area.

"What's going on B-More?" The lead rapper D-Boy, screamed into the microphone.

"I love you D-Boy." A girl in the crowd yelled out.

"I love you too baby." He responded. "But before we get this party started let's show some love to my man who made this all possible. B-More give it up for my man, the Prince of New York. Mr. Travon Outlaw."

The spotlight was put on the mystery man who was now no longer a mystery. The crowd gave him a standing ovation as he waived his hand in acceptance and quieted the crowd.

"Looks like we got us a business man ladies. Good luck to whoever gets that motherfucker." Monica said, sipping on her champagne.

"Okay. Now let's set this motherfucker off." D-Boy yelled to the top of his lungs.

Once again the crowd went crazy as the Realm Squad went into their new hit single *"Real thug shit"*. They were like pied pipers as the crowd moved to the music and headed to the dance floor and the stage area.

THE MEETING

TRAVON

"Yo Sincere where the chicks at?" I asked, looking around.

"Right over there." He responded, pointing to a table full of dimes.

"Gotdamn son, them bitches is bangin." I responded, showing my approval.

"C'mon baby. You already know how I get down." He replied,

"Yeah you a beast out here I'll give you that. I mean they all dimes at that table, but who is the one in the baby blue?" I asked, now not really caring about the rest.

"Oh. I'm not sure but I think she's the new girl. Monica told me about her. Her name is Tiffany or Veronica or some shit like that. Today is her first day in B-More. She just moved here from somewhere." Sincere informed me.

"Well these other chicks are hot, but I've got to have her. Make it happen fam." I instructed.

"Okay, but remember she's new so I don't know if she gets down like the rest of them." He warned me.

"I don't care. She's fucking beautiful, and if she doesn't get down like them then that's even better." I replied, with my mind set on meeting this woman.

"Okay. I'll put the word in." Sincere said, pulling out his I-phone.

I can't even describe her beauty in words. She was about 5'6 light skinned, about 135 pounds. She had long hair that came to the middle of her back. And the form fitting Juicy Couture outfit that she wore accen-

A Gangster's Melody 51

tuated her beautiful and flawless body. And while all of those things would grab any mans attention, none of it compared to her face. She had the face of a supermodel. I mean I had been with plenty of women from all over. But she was the true definition of a dime. And I had to have her.

"What are you doing?" I asked, as Sincere typed away on his I-Phone.

"I'm putting in a good word for you. Just the push of a button and presto. Now sit back and watch the magic happen." He instructed, as he pointed to the table of dimes.

"Well I'll be damned. Ain't this about a bitch?" Monica said, out loud looking at her Blackberry.

"What?" we all said, at the same time.

"Mr. Music mogul wants to meet Tiffany. I guess you're the lucky bitch tonight." Monica said, winking her eye at me and giving me a high five.

"Ain't this some shit? Your first night out and you score big. You lucky heffer." Terri added, jokingly.

"I'll drink to that." LaShawn joined in.

"I can't believe he picked me. Why me?" I asked, still a little shocked.

"Because you are a bad bitch that's why. Now stop questioning shit and get your confidence level up." Monica instructed, before we were interrupted by the waiter.

"Hello ladies. Mr. Outlaw asks two things. First, he'd like you to enjoy this bottle of *Louis the 13th*." He said, before being cut off by Terri.

"Louis the 13th? That nigga can't send no Kristal? I hate a broke nigga." she stated proudly.

"As a matter of fact maam. *Louis the 13th* is the club's finest Cognac. It retails at $3000 a bottle. *Kristal* on the other hand, is only $375..." The waiter stated matter of factly before continuing.

"He also asked that you be his guest at the private after party for The Realm Squad." He stated, politely.

"Hell yeah, tell him we'll be there." Monica stated.

"However maam. Mr. Outlaw requests your presence at his table now if you don't mind." The waiter stated, directing that statement to me.

"Damn. Private request and shit?" go ahead miss thing." Terri said, playfully hitting me on the arm.

"Oh, I don't know, um." I stuttered, until Monica cut me off.

"Girl if you don't get your silly ass up and go over there." She snapped.

I looked over in Travon's direction and he waived me over. As I reluctantly got up from my seat, Monica grabbed my hand.

"Remember everything we talked about." She reminded me.

"Okay I got you." I reassured her.

"Represent the SD's to the fullest girl." LaShawn yelled out.

As I walked over to his table, I could feel the butterflies doing 360 degree aerial stunts in my stomach. When he looked up and saw me approaching he dismissed the company that he had at the table and pulled out a chair for me.

"Hey what's up? My name is Tiffany" I said, nervously.

"Hey, how are you doing? My name is .."

"Travon Outlaw, I'm sure everybody in the club knows that by now." I said, cutting him off.

"Okay. You got jokes huh? That's what's up, beauty and a sense of humor." He replied, flashing a smile showing his white perfectly spaced and shaped teeth.

"So let me ask you something, out of all the women in here why did you ask *me* over to your table?" I asked, now loosening up a little bit.

A Gangster's Melody 53

"Well I could ask you the same thing, out of all the dudes in here why did you accept *my* invitation?" he replied, making a valid point.

"I guess we could be here all night going back and forth." I replied, avoiding his question.

"Okay. Well moving right along. So I hear you're new in town. About 24 hours now huh?" He asked, being inquisitive but hitting the nail on the head.

"Damn. How did you know that?" I asked, wondering how he had any information about me.

"Well when I'm interested in something or someone for that matter, I do my research." He responded, while pouring us both a drink.

"So why are you interested in me? How could you be interested in me? You don't even know me." I stated.

"Well since I don't know anything about you, all I have are a few things to go on right now. First and foremost are your looks. I mean I'm sure you hear that all day everyday all day but it is what it is. Second thing is I watched your reaction when the waiter asked you to come over here and you didn't jump at the opportunity and act all star struck and shit. You looked like you really ain't want to come over. And last but not least, you're new in town so you didn't have enough time to be corrupted by the local hood rats."

"Well I see you have done your research." I said, with a smile.

"Just a little. Now it's your turn. Why did you accept my invitation?" He asked, smiling back.

"Well I saw you when you walked in. I mean you just stood out. You look different, you dress different, and you carry yourself different. You just commanded so much attention when you entered the room and that's before anyone even knew who you were." I said, still blushing.

"Okay. So I see I'm not the only one that's been doing their research. That's what's up. So are you and your girls accepting my invite to my private after party tonight?" He said, taking a sip of his drink.

"I mean, I'm with it but if my girls don't go, then I don't go."

"So it's like that?" He asked.

"Yeah, stra'ight like that." I answered.

"I have a feeling your girls won't mind. D-boy and them can be pretty persuasive."

"Well like I said, it's up to them." I repeated.

"Well why wait? The guys are finishing up. Let's bounce."

The Realm Squad had finished their performance and headed stra'ight to our table after being swarmed by fans and groupies. I looked over at the table where the rest of my girls were sitting and noticed that each of them where engaged in a conversation with a man of their own. When D-boy and L.V. got to our table Travon stood up and congratulated them on a job well done.

"Ya'll niggas killed that shit as usual." Travon said, giving out dap and hugs to the group members.

"Yeah alright. Nigga how would you know? You was too busy politickin' with shorty." D-Boy said, giving me the once over.

"Yeah whatever son, I'm a business man, I can multi-task. Anyway, ya'll niggas ready to head back to the suite? " Travon replied.

"Nigga are you crazy? You see all these tricks and treats up in here?" D-boy replied, looking around at all of the scantily clad women.

"Don't worry, I got that covered." Travon reassured him.

"Alright man, you better have it covered." D-Boy replied.

A Gangster's Melody   55

After that was said we walked over to the table where Monica and the girls were sitting and they were still surrounded by men as if they were superstars. I mean they were literally hovering around them like a bunch of male groupies. I had never seen women garner so much attention in my life. I knew that being part of the Stiletto Divas would get me the same type of attention but I had mixed feelings about it. While I knew that it would have been very flattering I don't think I could have handled all of that attention. When Monica saw us approaching she dismissed the male groupies with a wave of her hand. And as if she were the black Queen of England the crowd dispersed on queue.

"So what's good?' Monica asked, looking Travon up and down.

"Well we were about to ask you and your girls the same thing." Travon replied.

"We're trying to hit up this after party that we keep hearing about." Monica said, pouring another glass of champagne.

"Good then. It's settled; let's get up out of here." Travon instructed.

We all gathered our belongings and headed outside to the parking lot where there was a white stretch limousine waiting with the chauffer holding the door open. Sincere, D-Boy, and L.V. ushered Monica, LaShawn, and Terri inside and just as I was about to climb in Travon stopped me.

"Why don't you ride with me in my car?" He asked, smiling at me.

"Oh no. I can't do that. I have to stay with my girls." I responded, remembering Monica's set of instructions.

"Girl, it's all good. Go ahead. We will meet you at the hotel." Monica said, totally contradicting the set of rules she had given me earlier.

"Well then I guess it's a done deal." Travon said, grabbing a hold of my hand.

"Okay. Where is your car?" I asked, nervously looking around the parking lot.

"It's right over there." He replied, pointing to a white Rolls Royce Phantom.

"Okay man, we're headed to the suite. We'll meet you there." D-Boy said, as the limo drove off.

As we walked across the parking lot towards Travon's car, I noticed all eyes on us by both haters and admirers. I even heard whispers of "Who's that bitch." But I paid it no mind I just smiled as Travon opened up the door of the Phantom so that I could get in.

"So why didn't we ride with them?" I asked, being curious.

"Because, I'm trying to get to know you. And with everything that's going to be going on later I might not get the chance to do that." He replied, climbing into the driver's seat.

When he started the car the soothing, sensual, sounds of R.Kelly came purring from the expensive stereo equipment in the Phantom. The first couple of minutes we drove in silence. I could also see that we didn't take the same route that the limousine had taken. I was a bit nervous but I tried not to show it. I was forced to break the ice when the fourth R. Kelly record came on in a row.

"Umm. Excuse me, but what does a thug nigga like you know about R.Kelly?" I asked, being funny but really wanting to know.

"Thug? What makes you think I'm a thug? And just for the record I might be R.Kelly's number one male fan. I mean come on; he's a musical genius. Now I'd never let him pick my daughter up from school, but he can work with my artists anytime." He replied, as we shared a light chuckle.

A Gangster's Melody

"So you have artists? What exactly do you do?"

"I manage singers, rappers, DJ's etc."

"Okay. That's what's up, so you know a lot of famous people huh?"

"I know a few people" he answered, modestly.

"Hmm. A nigga in your line of work must have pussy lined up around the corner." I stated matter of factly.

"Honestly, sometimes it's like that, but for the most part I don't pay those chicks no mind. I'll be honest, the whole groupie love thing, I've been there and done that. And that shit got real old, real fast. And I'm at a point in my life now where I want more than an occasional fuck or a one night stand." He replied, with sincerity seeping from his beautiful lips.

"Well it's good to know that you don't fit the stereotype." I responded.

"Well what about you Miss twenty-one questions. Where are you from and what brings you to the jungle?" He asked never taking his eyes off the road.

"There's not much to tell. Let's see, I'm from a small town in Ohio called Marion, I love doing hair and I just moved here yesterday to live with my grandmother because I just recently lost both of my parents."

"Damn shorty. I'm really sorry to hear that. But at least you still got your grand moms."

"Yeah right. I never really knew her too well. I mean I stayed a couple of summers as a kid but that was it. Now she's acting like I'm a total fucking stranger. We have been fighting since I got off the bus yesterday."

"Wow. That's crazy. Well how do you know those girls you were with?"

"Well you don't really want to know how we met, but Monica lives next door to my grandmother so we just clicked."

58 *Sean Wright*

"Okay. Well hopefully me and you can click too." He stated, with a smile on his face.

"We'll see Mr. Music Man." I responded, returning the smile.

For the next hour or so, Travon drove me around and gave me a tour of Baltimore. We talked and got to know each other. I liked him so far. He was handsome, smart, and successful, but most of all he had a good sense of humor. I can't count how many times he made me laugh as we drove around the streets of Baltimore. And I was in desperate need of a good laugh. My life seemed to be in shambles these past few weeks and I needed a good laugh to take the edge off. Talking to Travon made it seem like we knew each other forever. He told me about his childhood and I told him about mines. He was completely honest with me, and I was completely honest with him. Except for the story of how mommy and daddy died. I wasn't ready to tell anyone about that. And I probably never would. Travon went on to tell me how he and D-Boy had known each other since the fourth grade. And how they were more like brothers than friends. According to him, he was cool with the rest of the group too, but he and D-Boy had undying loyalty for one another. He even told me how D-boy jumped in front of a bullet for him a few years back when some haters tried to rob him for his necklace. He went on to say that D-Boy almost died, and that is why as long as he lived he would always take care of D-Boy. By the time we pulled up to the hotel, I was convinced that I wanted to see Travon again. And I swear it had nothing to do with his money, or his fame. He was genuine and I liked that. As we pulled into the hotel parking lot I automatically knew which suite was his from the loud music and all the noise that was coming from the room. When we en-

A Gangster's Melody 59

tered the room, there were our friends indulging in weed, alcohol, and God knows what else.

"It's about time you got here nigga." Sincere yelled out, with a blunt in his hand.

"Tiffany are you good baby?" Monica shouted, also inhaling a puff of weed smoke.

"Yeah. I'm stra'ight. I didn't have to smack him up." I responded, playfully punching Travon in the arm.

"Yo Tray, let me holler at you real quick." D-Boy said, getting Travon's attention as they both disappeared into the kitchen area.

***

"What's good fam?" Travon asked.

"Yo. I just spoke to homeboy in D.C. and he's going to need another one of those packages."

"Damn. I just gave you that package earlier."

"Yeah I told him that. He said that one is gone already."

"Ya'll niggas is killing me."

"Shit, you should be happy that they're selling this fast."

"Yeah I guess you're right. I'll square you up tomorrow before I leave, but this is a big order. Don't fuck this up."

"Nigga do I ever fuck up? Now let's get back to partying with them hoes. You know them bitches is some freaks right? The girl Terry already gave me and L.V. some head. And Sincere was sucking the other two's titties and shit. You better go get you some."

"Nah, I'm good. I already got the one I want. Ya'll niggas have fun."

"I feel you. The one you bagged looks way better than the others. Let me know when you done. I want to get a crack at that."

"Nah, Chill. She ain't like that. Trust me."

"What you mean she ain't like that? She down with them bitches ain't she?"

"Yo nigga. She ain't like that alright?"

"Alright nigga, whatever. But I ain't never known you to handcuff no bitch." D-Boy stated, before leaving and returning to the party.

"So what does a girl have to do to get a drink around here?" I yelled, jokingly.

"I got you ma. What you want?" D-Boy said, jumping in front of Travon.

"It don't matter, surprise me. Just don't make it too strong." I said.

"Alright ma. I'll be right back." He said, smiling flirtatiously.

While I waited on D-Boy to bring my drink back, I just mingled and laughed with everyone else that was in the room. I saw Monica disappear into one of the bedrooms with L.V. and lord only knows what was about to go down. These girls were definitely wild and crazy. But hey, who was I to judge? We were all enjoying ourselves, and while I was now an honorary Stiletto Diva member, I was still so much different from them. I knew I was way out of my league, but I refused to let the company that I kept define who I was as a person. Besides, like I told Mama Belle, I was old enough to know right from wrong. And as long as I could kick it with the "in" crowd and have fun without getting into any trouble, then there was no harm, and no foul. And with that being said, I accepted my drink from D-Boy and continued to party the night away.

As the night progressed I drank and enjoyed myself like I never had before. We all laughed and joked on one another. All except Travon, who had been in his bedroom by himself for the past hour or so. The rest of us drank, smoked and just had fun. D-Boy kept me company while Travon's rude ass was in his bedroom

A Gangster's Melody 61

on his damn cell phone. But so what? I was having way too much fun to give a shit. D-boy and I were laughing and dancing, and I could feel the room starting to spin as he continued to make me drinks at my request. D-Boy had grabbed me by my hand and was leading me somewhere when Travon came out of his bedroom and stopped us.

"Where are ya'll going?" Travon asked, looking at the both of us.

"We are going to get a little privacy." D-Boy responded, sharply.

"Oh word? It's like that? That's what's up?" Travon said, shooting me a cold stare that showed his disapproval.

"Travon wait." I said, subconsciously slurring my speech. Before taking a step towards him and falling flat on my face.

"Oh shit. That bitch is fucked up." Sincere said, laughing and coming out of the kitchen.

"Come on ma. You had a little too much to drink." Travon said, picking me up and carrying me into his bedroom. Once inside his bedroom he laid me down on the bed and got a cold washcloth from bathroom and wiped my forehead gently.

"Travon, I'm fucked up. The room is spinning, and I didn't even drink that much either." I said, with my speech now almost inaudible.

"It's alright Tiffany. Just lay here for a while and get your mind right. Once you get your bearings back I will have my limo take you home. I'll be back in a few minutes to check on you." He said, getting up to leave the room.

"Wait, Travon. Don't leave yet. The fucking room is still spinning." I said, pulling him back down onto the bed. Once I pulled him down, we were face to face. And I couldn't help the feeling that came over me. Un-

62   *Sean Wright*

characteristically, I leaned up and kissed Travon, and he returned the gesture. Things started to heat up as I felt a feeling take over my body that I had never felt before. It's as if I went numb with every touch. And every ounce of his breath that hit my body sent a tingly sensation throughout every nerve in my body. My womanhood began to gush and overflow with happiness and I could feel it running down my leg. This was crazy. Was it possible for foreplay to make you feel this way? I guess it was. I don't know what came over me, but I had to have him. In between short pants of breath I managed to spit out.

"Tray wait. Do you have any condoms?"

"Most definitely." He answered. And with that said he rolled over to his left and pulled a box of condoms out of the night table drawer. In one swift motion he had dropped his pants to the floor and helped me out of my clothes as well. When we were both naked, we both stood still and salivated for a second. Him, over the fact that my body was tight and my 38 DD's stood erect without a bra, and me over the fact that his manhood stood at attention and had a slight curve in it. When he could take no more of just watching me Travon placed the condom on his massive pole and slid it into me nice and slow. I dug my freshly manicured nails into his back as he penetrated my tight wet pussy with every inch of his throbbing love muscle, which I figured to be somewhere between 9 or 10 inches. With every stroke, I winced in pain and at times found myself biting softly on his shoulder blade to brace myself for the next stroke. Travon, was truly a master in the bedroom. When he was done proving his skills in the missionary position, he instructed me to turn over and get on all fours, which I did without any hesitation. I buried my face in the expensive goose down pillows as he grabbed my waist and penetrated me slowly from

A Gangster's Melody 63

the back. Each stroke and every touch set off the alarms in my erogenous zones. I completely lost track of all my senses, and apparently my religion too as I called out for God, Allah, Buddha, or anyone I could thank for me getting this serving. Hell, at this point I would praise a head of cabbage named Ralph if I knew it was responsible for me meeting Travon. The pleasure seemed like it went on forever and with every position that Travon twisted and put me in, I was sure to orgasm about 3 times each. But it was the Grand Finale that would open up the floodgates to my love canal and send me into a deep slumber. Travon instructed me to lie on my back, spread my legs and clothes my eyes. Again, I did as I was told. And it was then that he gave me oral pleasure that I will never forget. As he gently placed kisses on my clit, and sucked it until it got rock hard and began to throb in his mouth, I took turns clawing the sheets and his back. I was definitely in a state of bliss, and when he stuck his finger in my mouth and then into my pussy and pushed the button on my G-spot, that's when I exploded, screamed his name and instantly fell asleep.

When I woke up Travon was passed out next to me and as the time on the clock began to come into focus I could see that it read 4:13 am. I quickly jumped up, temporarily ignoring the hangover, or the pain that shot through my body with every move. I began to shake Travon.

"Travon wake up." I said, shaking him slightly but I got no response.

"Come on Travon. I have to get home." I said a little louder and shaking him much harder this time.

"Okay. Okay. I'm getting up. Go get your peoples together so I can have my driver take you home." He mumbled, still half asleep. I quickly put my clothes on and stumbled into the living room only to find that everyone had left. How could they have left me there? What about Monica's rules and the Stiletto Divas commandments and all of that other shit? I would deal with that later but now I had to get home fast. Travon came stumbling into the living room behind me.

"Damn. Where's everybody at?" He asked, just as shocked as I was.

"I don't know, but I have to get home now. My grandmother is going to flip the fuck out." I said, with tears of anger welling up in my eyes.

"Okay. I'll take you. Let's go." He replied, grabbing his car keys.

We rode in silence all the way back to Mama Belle's house. Travon may have been speaking to me, but I was so upset I completely tuned him out. I was mad at Monica for leaving me, I was mad at the fact that I was in pain, and I was really mad at the fact that I had allowed myself to get into the situation where I would have to hear Mama Belle's mouth in the morning. When we pulled up in front of the house Travon reached over to hug me and I instinctively jumped and pulled away from him.

"I have your number Travon. I will call you." I said, sounding colder than I wanted to. But even after me giving him the cold shoulder he was a gentleman and waited to see if I made it into the house safe. As I got closer to the porch I could see that there was a note on the door. I tried to open the screen door but it was locked. The note read: *"I put this note on the door at 2:38 am. Your hot ass should have been in the house by then. So wherever you been at, you better go back there. And you better not ring my gotdamn doorbell."* Obviously the key she gave me didn't fit the screen door. Now I was really pissed.

"Fucking bitch." I screamed as I headed back to the car.

A Gangster's Melody 65

"Are you Okay baby?" Travon asked, seeing that I was visibly upset.

"My grandmother locked me out the fucking house. I only been here one day and I hate it already." I yelled, as I started to cry.

"Come on get in. You can come back to the suite with me and I'll bring you back later." He said, opening the door for me. I hesitated a minute before accepting the offer. Then I got in the car and we pulled off.

"Okay. That's what's up. We can go back to the suite. Get started on round two, then I can take you to breakfast and then home." Travon said, grinning from ear to ear.

"Look. It ain't goinig to be no fucking round two okay? If that's what you feel then just leave me right here and I will take my chances ringing the motherfucking doorbell." I spat back at him.

"Ok baby. Calm down. What's the matter?" Travon asked, with a confused look on his face.

"I'm not sure, because I don't remember much. But I'm pretty sure you took advantage of me while I was drunk." I stated, angrily. Travon quickly pulled the car over and slammed on the brakes.

"Hold on. Take advantage of you? Yeah right. *You* started kissing *me* and that's what set it all off. You only stopped me once, and that was to ask me if I had a condom. I said yeah, and that was that. Believe me Tiffany, I don't have to take or sneak pussy from nobody. Never have, never will. So don't flatter your motherfucking self. Would you have been saying the same thing if I let you go in the bathroom with D-Boy?" Travon screamed, now he too was visibly upset.

"D-Boy? What are you talking about?" I asked, confused.

"Oh, now you don't remember? How convenient." He shot back at me.

"Travon, I really have no idea what you are talking about." I said, now starting to worry.

"Whatever." He said, looking at me with disgust as if he wanted to spit in my face.

"Whatever? What the fuck do you mean whatever? I don't know what kind of bitch you think I am, but this is not how I wanted to lose my virginity mother-fucker." I yelled, now starting to cry again.

"Virginity? Look ma I'm.." Travon tried to speak but I cut him off.

"Look. I don't want to talk about it. Just drive okay?" I said, as he pulled off and I leaned my head against the window and cried heavily. Travon held my hand as he drove. This time I didn't pull away. I just cried silently as we headed back to the hotel. When we arrived at the hotel I hurried inside and eased down on the couch, still in a lot of pain.

"Can I get you anything?" Travon asked, with the utmost sincerity in his voice.

"I just want to soak in a nice hot bath and lie down." I replied, with a hint of appreciation.

"Okay. I'll get you a towel. Do you need anything else?" He asked.

"No thank you. I'm good. As a matter of fact, some shorts and a t-shirt will be good." I responded. Travon handed me a washcloth and a towel.

"Here you go. I'll have the shorts and the t-shirt waiting for you when you get out. If you look under the sink, there is some complimentary Aromatherapy bubble bath and bath beads and all sorts of shit. Help yourself to whatever is in the suite." Travon instructed, once again, sounding so sincere.

"Thank you." I said, as I headed to the bathroom, Travon poured a drink and answered his cell phone. He told me it was Sincere and that he would find out what happened to everybody. Then he went into his

A Gangster's Melody   67

bedroom and closed the door. I ran a nice hot bath and turned on the Jacuzzi jets. I then helped myself to the Aromatherapy products that Travon told me about. I eased into the tub nice and slow and winced in pain from the combination of boiling hot water and the sudden loss of my virginity. Once my body got acclimated to the hot water I laid back, put a hot rag over my eyes and just tried to relax and figure out what the hell was going on with my life. How could my life take such a drastic turn in just a matter of hours? In less than 24 hours I was damn near stabbed by a group of the local fly girls, then I was befriended by the same group of girls, then I was treated to a shopping spree and makeover, rubbed elbows with celebrities and lost my virginity to a very attractive, and successful man. What the hell was going on? After just soaking for a while I removed the rag from my eyes so that I could wash up. I looked at the water and to my surprise there were droplets of blood in the water from where I was ripped from my little *sex-capade* with Travon. Well no use crying over spilled milk. What's done is done, I thought to myself. I was finished in the tub and felt a whole lot better. Travon had never brought me the shorts and t-shirt so I wrapped a towel around me and walked to his bedroom. He was still on the phone with Sincere. When he saw my reflection in the mirror, he cut his phone call short.

"Yo Sincere. I'll holler at you later and we'll make some power moves. Alright fam. Peace." He said as he closed his cell phone, before turning and talking to me.

"Hey I couldn't find any shorts to fit you, but feel free to get a t-shirt out of the closet." He said pointing to the giant walk-in closet.

"Thank you. Damn. How long are you in town for?" I asked, noticing the abundance of clothes he had hanging up in the closet.

"Just a few more days, but I change a couple of times a day." he responded laughing.

"Yeah. I can see that." I said, putting on one of his oversized t-shirts.

"Well I'm going to hit the couch, the bedroom is all yours." He said, grabbing a pillow and a blanket.

"Well wait, that bath woke me up a bit. Why don't we talk for a minute?" I asked, patting the bed.

"I don't know ma? No disrespect, but that's how shit got started earlier." He said, hesitant about my offer.

"Look. I don't know what happened earlier, but I wasn't in my right state of mind. And I apologize for blaming you. The night is really a blank." I said, apologetically.

"It's all good. I didn't mean to scream on you either, but as funny as it may sound, I'm really feeling you so far and I don't want you to think nothing negative about me." He said, inching closer to the bed.

"Come on, let's call a truce." I said, smiling and pretending to wave a white flag.

"A truce huh? Okay. So what's up?" he said, finally sitting down.

"Nothing really. I just don't want to hear my grandmother's mouth that's all." I said.

"Let's not talk about that right now." He said, playing in my hair as I lay across his lap.

"Well what do you want to talk about then?" I asked, feeling relaxed.

"I don't know. Tell me something good. Tell me what your dreams are." He asked, inquisitively.

"Well I have a lot, but my biggest dream is to own a chain of beauty salons." I answered, proudly.

"Really? That's what's up. What's another one?"

A Gangster's Melody 69

"Nah. I'm not telling you that, because you're going to think that I'm just saying that because of your line of work."

"Come on, tell me. What is it?" He urged on.

"Okay. I want to be a singer."

"Say word. Let me hear you blow something."

"Oh hell no. You crazy Tray."

"Come on. You know if the shit is hot I can put you on, so don't blow your chance being shy."

"So if I do good you're going to hook me up?" I asked, sitting up.

"You already know." He answered.

"Okay. Here I go." I said, standing up and going into my best rendition of Mary J. Blige's "Real Love". Yes. I had stood up and sang my heart out like I was a finalist on American Idol. I had my eyes closed and I was really feeling it. I was hitting the high notes and bouncing around and shit. You couldn't tell me nothing. When the song was done I opened up my eyes and tried to stop myself from breathing heavy.

"So what do you think?" I asked, all excited about my new record deal.

"Keeping it real ma? I think we need to start on that chain of beauty salons asap." Travon said, bursting out with laughter.

"Fuck you Travon." I yelled, jokingly as I grabbed a pillow and hit him over the head with it. Travon grabbed another pillow and returned the playful assault. We wrestled and played around on the bed until Travon was on top of me, and our eyes met once again. And once again I was mesmerized by the glow in his chestnut brown eyes. I leaned up to kiss him and he pulled away.

"Nah chill. We ain't going through that again." He said.

"No it's Okay. I know what I'm doing this time. Just be careful please" I reassured him, before pulling him back down to continue our kiss. Travon made love to me for the next hour or so until we fell asleep. Once again, I was the first one to wake up. I looked at the clock and it was 9:17am. I woke Travon up and he got dressed and took me home. This time we didn't ride in silence, we laughed, joked and stole sensual kisses in between red lights. It seemed like we had known each other forever. I had never had a real boyfriend before and I guess it's because my daddy was the epitome of what a real man was, and I held every man to those standards. And although it was still very early, Travon was coming damn close to those standards so far.

ALL HELL BREAKS LOOSE

When we pulled up in front of Mama Belle's house I was smiling from ear to ear as a result of the conversation Travon and I shared on the ride home. I knew that when I got in the house I would have to deal with Mama Belle's mouth. But I was on cloud nine and nothing she could say or do could bring me down. I already had it in my mind to be very apologetic and head to my room. I knew I would have to tune out all the ranting, raving and the preaching. She really killed me with the preaching shit. For her to be so holy and the poster child for the world's best sanctified Christian, she sure did a lot of hypocritical shit. The yelling, the cursing, the demeaning ways that she speaks, and let's not forget the shacking up with Mr. Rufus. But anyway, she would have to answer that whenever she met the man upstairs. As we pulled up I noticed that both the main door and the screen door were open.

"Well let me go in and face the music." I said, taking a deep breath.

"If you need me just hit me on my cell." Travon instructed, grabbing my hand.

"Okay. I will." I responded. When I got out of the car and headed up the walkway Travon stopped me.

"Hey." He yelled out, causing me to turn around and stick my head back in the car. "You know you're too old to be going through this right?" He said.

"What other choice do I have?" I said, shrugging my shoulders and walking away. As I got closer to the house I could hear Mama Belle screaming and yelling. When I got to the screen door I just eavesdropped and listened as she continued her tirade. What I heard next would cut through me like a hot knife through warm butter.

"I don't give a damn what her excuse is. She ain't been here but a hot minute and she causing nothing but grief already." Mama Belle yelled out.

"Lula Belle, you have to take into consideration all that the child has been through recently." Mr.Rufus responded, trying to defend me.

"What she has been through? What about me? A parent shouldn't outlive her child. Now because of that whore my son called his wife, my baby boy is dead."

"Come on now Belle, that ain't right. That's your granddaughter's mother you're talking about. " Mr. Rufus said, trying to calm her down.

"That's what they say Rufus, but I ain't never believe that bold faced lie that little Puerto Rican heffer Marisol told my son. Now don't get me wrong, I'm sorry she's dead, both her and my son. But that little girl don't look no more like my son Leroy than the man on the moon. I'm only taking her in because I knew Leroy would have wanted it that way."

"Now Belle, you stop talking about your kinfolk like that and hush up all that foolishness."

"Rufus I done told you that little bitch ain't no kin to me. And my son was a fool to believe anything else. And besides it's the truth. Her mother was a fucking whore and the apple don't fall far from the tree because her daughter is a fucking whore too." She said, slamming something down. By this time my eyes were red and flooded with tears and I had heard enough. I flung the screen door open and stormed through the house in a rampage. I headed stra'ight for the kitchen where all of the commotion was coming from. Mama Belle and Rufus froze in mid sentence as I rounded the corner into the kitchen. I made a B-Line stra'ight for Mama Belle.

A Gangster's Melody   73

"Let me tell you something you mean old bitch, you say one more thing about my mother or my father and I'm going to forget the age difference and whoop your old ass up in here." I yelled, pointing my finger in her face.

"Tiffany calm down baby." Mr.Rufus said, grabbing my waist. I instinctively grabbed a knife from the dish rack and turned to him.

"Get the fuck off of me you perverted motherfucker." I said, pointing the butcher knife in his face. Mr.Rufus turned on his heels and ran out of the house. I turned my attention back to Mama Belle. I pointed the knife in her face and I was crying hysterically.

"You ain't nothing but the devil, how dare you threaten your own grandmother?" She said, grabbing her chest and crying.

"Oh now you're my grandmother? Bitch you trippin." I screamed in her face. I believe I may have lost total control and pounced on her if Monica wouldn't have come running into the kitchen and grabbed me from behind.

"Yo chill Tiffany. What are you doing? Calm down. Let's go to my house for a little while." Monica said, trying to calm me down.

"A little while my ass. You better pack your little funky ass bags and go over there for good." Mama Belle screamed, now getting gangster because Monica was holding me back. I kicked and screamed trying to get away from Monica.

"Bitch I'll kill you up in here. Say something else about my parents. I fucking dare you." I screamed in anger. As Monica dragged me out of the house, Mama Belle followed behind us, talking shit and antagonizing me.

"Go on now Ms. Lula Belle. I'll be back for her things." Monica stated, still trying to hold me back.

"You better come back and get them or that shit will be in the garbage." Mama Belle spat back.

Monica dragged me kicking and screaming to her house. The neighbors were all outside being nosy, until Monica told them to mind their business. Monica forced me into her house and up the stairs before she let me go.

"Girl what the fuck happened? I'm over here smoking and shit, and Mr. Rufus ran over here talking about you going crazy with a knife and shit." Monica said, looking all confused.

"You don't understand, I overheard that bitch talking real dirty about my mother. Really fucking dirty. Calling her a whore and saying that I'm not my daddy's baby and all that shit." I responded, still pacing back and forth in anger.

"Okay girl calm down. You're going to bust a fucking blood vessel. If you know it's not the truth, then fuck what she said. You know, sticks and stones and all that other shit." Monica said, jokingly trying to calm me down.

"Look that's easy for you to say, I wouldn't even be in this mess if you wouldn't have fucking left me at that fucking hotel. So fuck you, fuck the Stiletto Divas and fuck your fake ass rules." I screamed, pointing my finger in her face.

"Okay. First of all, stop yelling and disrespecting my crib, second of all stop yelling and disrespecting me, and third of all get your motherfucking hand out of my face before I drop you right where you stand." She said, through clinched teeth. She waited for me to move my hand before she continued.

"Now, if you must know we tried to tell you we were leaving, but from all the moaning and screaming you were doing we figured you didn't want to be disturbed so we bounced. I told you before we went out

A Gangster's Melody 75

that I wasn't no fucking babysitter and that's what the fuck I meant. Now because you are all emotional right now, I'm going to forget the shit you just pulled with me. But be warned Tiffany, this is your only freebie. Next time we gonna rip it up, and it won't be any love lost because SD's fight all the time. Now I have to make a run real quick, you stay here, cool the fuck off, and make yourself at home. Since it looks like this will be your home for a little while." She said, grabbing a set of car keys.

"Shit Monica. With everything I just went through, and everything that happened last night. I just want to sleep it off." I said, now feeling bad that I snapped on her.

"Oh yeah little miss innocent. When I get back you can fill me in on exactly what happened last night with you and Mr. Outlaw. I got a call from Sincere and from what I understand Travon is really feeling you. So take a nap and relax until I get back because I want the full scoop." She said, smiling.

"What did he say?" I asked, blushing wanting more feedback.

"Bitch I'm already late fucking with you, we'll talk later. And stay the fuck away from your grandmother's house." She instructed.

"Okay. Okay. I promise." I responded.

"Oh yeah. If the phone rings, don't answer it. I'll be back soon." She said as she rushed out of the house.

GETTING ADJUSTED

After the fallout at Mama Belle's I knew my life was about to take yet another drastic turn. Monica had told me I could stay with her as long as I wanted, and that was all fine and dandy, but this Stiletto Diva lifestyle was going to take some getting used to. Over the past few weeks I was subjected to hearing Monica's late night sex sessions with either a man a woman or herself. The bedroom I slept in was right on the other side of hers and both of our beds lay against the wall, so there was no escaping the noise. I won't lie. A few times it sounded so good that I pleasured myself while imagining it being me and Travon on the other side of the wall getting it in. He and I had gone out a few more times since the first night we met. Each date was more memorable and spectacular than the last. We had eaten down by the water at the Baltimore Harbor; we had gone to DC, Virginia, and Philadelphia. Travon said he didn't like to stay local too much. And I didn't care because I was having the time of my life. Doing things I had never done before and seeing places and things I had only seen on TV. It had been a few days since I last saw him though because he had gone back to New York, but that didn't stop the communication. Travon had made me throw away that pre-paid phone that Ms. Gloria was so nice to get for me and he went and got me the brand new Blackberry equipped with all the features. He said that he needed me to be able to pick the phone up whenever I wanted to and not just after nine when the minutes were free. It's like our conversation was never ending. We would stay up all night on the phone either until the sun came up or until one of us fell asleep. We also shared intimate and deep secrets with one another. Travon told me how he was in his last year of Law School when a family emergency caused him to drop out unexpectedly. He said that since then he had been going strong with the music business, and apparently it had been paying off really well. I never imagined my Baltimore experience would be like this.

"You ready girl?" Monica asked, interrupting my thoughts.

"You already know" I responded, getting up from the couch and straightening my clothes.

"Aight let's be out."

We left the house, got in Monica's car for the day and headed to the mall to meet up with Lashawn and Terri. As Monica navigated the Audi 8 down the Baltimore expressway Travon and I exchanged silly little text messages back and forth. I must have really been lost in my own thoughts because apparently Monica had been talking and I hadn't heard a word of what she said.

"So what do you think about that?" She asked.

"Yeah that's what's up." I responded, pretending that I heard what she said. Just then Monica abruptly pulled the car over to the shoulder and slammed it into park.

"Okay, take 'em off." She said, looking at me.

"Take what off?" I responded, confused as hell.

"Your clothes, you just said that I could fuck you right now if I pulled over."

"What? Girl stop playing." I responded, embarrassed that it was now confirmed that I was paying her no mind as she spoke.

"Yeah exactly. You aint heard a damn word I said. You all wrapped up in that damn phone and shit." She said, as she pulled off back into the traffic.

"Girl stop trippin, aint nothing wrong with me and Tray texting back and forth. What's the big deal?"

A Gangster's Melody 79

"The problem is, you going soft over this nigga, I mean I have been taking you everywhere, introducing you to some real official cats. And you aint even giving them the time of day cause you all open off that next nigga."

"Goin soft? Let's not forget I'm still in Diva training. And besides, what's wrong with me actually liking Travon and not just wanting him for his money?"

"Liking him? Aww shit. It's time to de-program and then re-program. Bitch you trippin hard. You are breaking the golden rule. Whatever you do, don't let the girls hear you say no crazy shit like that or you'll never hear the end of it."

"Shit. Aint no shame in my game. Besides, they already know. They both tried to call me last night but I told them that I was on the phone with him. They talked shit about it until they got the dial tone." I said, laughing out loud.

"Girl you is out back. But don't worry. I'mma tighten ya square ass up." We both laughed as Monica dodged in and out of traffic. When we got to the mall Terri and Lashawn were standing out front flirting with some guys that were passing by.

"Let's go bitches. We got work to do." Monica instructed, as she walked right passed them without even stopping. And just as they were instructed they followed suit. Once inside the mall we congregated near the mall directory.

"Okay, so today we hit Top Fashions. It's the new store right next to Macy's. They got everything in there. Gucci, Louis, Prada, Coogie and mad accessories. They only got one guard on the door. He's a bald-head fat dude. His name is Kurt. We went to school together. Ya'll already know what that's hitting for. And behind the counter is a chick I picked up the other night who is going to pretend not to see a thing. I will handle Kurt. Lashawn and Terri you hit the racks, and Tiffany you sit back and watch and make sure we don't get booked." Monica directed, and as if we were in a football huddle we listened to her quarterback the plays and then broke the huddle to go and execute.

When we got to the store everything was just as Monica said it would be. The store was full of top designer clothes. The girl was behind the counter. And there was Kurt, sitting his big ass on a stool by the door salivating at the site of us entering the cash cow he should have been guarding.

"Oh my God. Kurtis Ramsey is that you? I don't believe it. It's been years." Monica said, pretending to be excited to see her old friend.

"Gotdamn Monica. You looking even better now than you did in school." Kurt responded, getting up giving Monica a hug taking advantage of the opportunity to feel her ass.

While Monica and Kurt continued reminiscing, Terri and Lashawn made a B-Line straight for the clothes racks. I watched from afar and attempted to learn. My only question was where were they going to put the stolen items. They each only had their pocketbooks. My questions were answered as they quickly moved through the aisles stuffing item after item into their bags. I wasn't sure how it was all fitting. They made the pocketbooks look like circus clown cars. I was amazed at how swift and precise they were as the cleaned up rack after rack. I wandered through the aisles pretending to be interested in purchasing something; I noticed a Dolce and Gabanna blouse that was hot as hell. I looked at the $800 price tag and immediately understood why they were stealing this shit. The designers were robbing us blind so why not get them back. Terri saw me eying the blouse and winked at me letting me know that it would soon be mines.

A Gangster's Melody 81

And in less than 15 minutes it was all over. Lashawn came out of the Gucci section and signaled that the shopping spree was over.

"Man these prices are way too fucking high. Why they got a store like this in the hood knowing we can't afford this shit? I'm out yo!" Lashawn ranted, pretending not to be interested in anything in the store.

"Well Kurt it's been nice chopping it up with you but I gotta roll out."Monica said, ending her fake conversation with Kurt.

"Well hold up Monica. Maybe we can exchange numbers and grab a bite to eat or something." Kurt said, trying his luck.

"Well Kurt, I do have a man but I tell you what. Now that I know you work here I will stop by and see you every free chance I get okay boo?" Monica said, kissing him on his cheek as he melted like butter. And before he could respond we were gone.

Back at Monica's house we all gathered in the living room as Terri and Lashawn began to unload the stash. I watched in amazement as they proceeded to pull thousands of dollars worth of shirts, jeans and accessories out of the tiny handbags. They then continued to make two separate piles. One was for us, and the other was to sell on the street. Even with the 50% off street value there was still well over ten grand. Now I was beginning to see how they stayed so fly and in fashion. My mouth salivated at the thought of my pretty ass being draped in all the hottest gear. I was still amazed at how quick and efficient this band of beautiful thieves were.

"Here you go newbie." Terri said as she slid a large pile of clothes my way.

"Good lookin out girl" I said, as I held one of the many expensive blouses up to my chin.

"No problem girl, you one of us now so I gotta look out for you like all sisters look out for each other. Matter of fact I'll tell you what. I will trade you three of these Gucci outfits for that nigga Travon's number." Terri responded.

"No thank you. I wouldn't trade his number for all the hot shit in that store."

"Shit. You might as well before he fucks one of us and you don't get nothing out the deal." Lashawn added.

"Nah. Trust me Travon aint like that. He would never even play me like that." I responded, defending Travon as if I had known him forever.

"Bitch you trippin. They all like that. And the sooner you get that through your pretty yet ditzy head the better." Monica jumped in, semi-scolding me.

"Whatever. Anyway what's next on the agenda for today?" I asked eager to change the subject.

"Well we gonna throw that shit on and head down to the park, they got the summer league basketball tournaments starting today. That's shit is gonna be packed." Monica said.

"Yeah nothing but money all over the place." Terri confirmed.

"Well what are we waiting for? Let's get this shit poppin. And Tiffany you better not strike out today. Make momma proud." Monica said, patting me on my ass.

"Okay, Okay. I got you." I agreed, reluctantly.

"Good, now you get in the shower and get dressed first, since you always take the longest to get ready. Ya'll two meet us back here in an hour." Monica instructed, as we all did as we were told.

SHOOTING THE BREEZE

When we got to the park it was just as the girls had described it. There were people everywhere. It looked just like the club parking lot the first night we went out but this was even bigger and better, because of the size of the park. I saw all sorts of cars from Benzes, to Bentleys. There were Range Rovers and motorcycles on deck, and thousands of people mingling and waiting for the games to start. Monica had managed to get us a Range Rover for the day as well. When we pulled up, all eyes were on us as usual. The niggas was loving us and the bitches were either hating or wanted to be down with us. In any event I was loving the attention I was getting in the Gucci coochie cutters and matching bra top with the heels to match. I had to ever so often re-arrange my 38 double D's so that they wouldn't come flying out of the bra top that was supposed to hold them snug.

"Okay bitches, this is it. I smell at least a couple hundred stacks up in here today so a good percentage of that should come home with us. Ya dig?" Monica said to the rest of us.

"Oh you already know you aint got to tell me twice I already seen a few prospects." Lashawn responded.

"Yeah me too." Terri joined in.

"And what about my prized pupil, you spot anything yet?" Monica asked me.

"Yeah I seen a couple candidates." I lied, not wanting anyone but Travon.

"Alright then, let's spread out and get this money. Keep ya'll phones on." Monica instructed, as we all went our separate ways.

A Gangster's Melody

I hadn't got a good six steps away when I was approached by this tall chocolate athletic guy that kind of resembled Morris Chestnut.

"Hey Shawty. What's ya name?" He asked, smiling showing his diamond encrusted teeth.

"My name is Tiffany." I replied, hoping he would just keep it moving.

"What's good? My name is Breeze." He said, extending his hand.

"Nice to meet you." I responded, shaking his hand.

"I aint never seen you round here before, I would remember a dime like you trust me."

"Yeah well I aint been here that long. I'm new in town."

"Oh okay. That's what's up. Are you new enough to still be single?" He asked, making his move.

"Um something like that." I responded, subconsciously looking him up and down checking out his attire.

"Oh baby don't let the basketball shorts and t-shirt fool you. I'm only wearing this because I got a game in a few minutes. And after I win that game I'm gonna pick you up in that Bentley right over there and we are gonna go shopping and out to dinner. Put my number in your phone. "He instructed, as I pulled my phone out.

"210-555-6969 as soon as the game is over just hit me. We'll go back to my condo, I'll take a shower, get changed and then we'll be out."

"Okay slow down. One thing at a time. Let's see if I call you first."

"Why wouldn't you?" He said arrogantly, flashing his diamond teeth again. Which I now saw spelled out his name.

"Anyway. Maybe I'll holler at you later. Then again maybe I won't." I teased.

"Yeah okay. We'll see youngin." He replied, in his Baltimore drawl as I sashayed away.

I had wandered around for about 30 minutes or so accepting and rejecting phone numbers from niggas lobbying for a piece of my pie. I had only taken the numbers for show and tell with the girls. Travon was proving to be all I ever wanted and needed. But to hear the girls tell it, all niggas was the same and they would never change so their motto was "do it to them first and do it to them worst." And that's the creed they lived by. But unlike them I knew a great man who was the total opposite of everything they claimed that men stood for. My daddy was nothing like the sex craved monsters they made all men out to be.

"Hey girl, how you lookin?" Monica said, sneaking up behind me.

"I'm doin pretty good I guess. I bagged a nigga with a Bentley."

"Who? The only nigga in this park with a Bentley is that nigga Breeze. You bagged him?"

"Yup. I sure did." I responded, now feeling myself.

"Damn girl that's what's up. That nigga there got his shit together. I don't even know why he out here getting all sweaty and shit. He is way too smooth for that."

"He talkin about taking me shopping and out to eat right after the game."

"Yeah he about to spend a grip on you, damn you are one lucky bitch. Yo, call that nigga and have him get us some seats right near the bench so we can watch the game. The game he playin in is gonna be good. Them niggas is playin for like $250,000."

"Damn, that much for some basketball?"

"Yeah, it ain't trickin if you got it."

I pulled my cell phone out and called Breeze like Monica asked me to do. And as if he knew I would

A Gangster's Melody 87

call, he already had a seat waiting for me. I just had to get him to clear a space for Monica and the girls. We had all gathered and attempted to watch the game amidst all of the niggas trying to hit on us in between plays. I watched as Breeze made his way up and down the court scoring points at will as if he played in the NBA. He was phenomenally good; it kind of made me wonder why he chose the streets over going pro. The other team couldn't keep up. Either he was shooting a jump shot, or slam dunking the ball. When they tried to double team him, he did some type of fancy pass. Each move excited the crowd to the tune of oooo's and ahhhh's. During half time, Breeze came and talked with me for a while before rejoining his team in the huddle. The second half proved to be no different from the first. There was Breeze, B-More's very own Michael Jordan scoring at will, rendering his opponents defenseless. When the final buzzer rang it was a massacre. Breeze's team 128 the losers 88. The winners congregated at center court holding up trophies and celebrating their victory, as a man in a suit and tie grabbed the microphone and quieted the crowd. He gave a quick speech about everyone coming out and showing unity and then presented Breeze with a giant MVP trophy. Breeze then gave his quick acceptance speech and walked towards me with the trophy winking and smiling. I'm sure he was thinking about what he was going to do to me, or what he thought he was going to do to me. Just as I was thinking about spending his money. But neither thought would come to fruition, when Breeze was about twenty steps away from me I saw someone coming up behind him, who I assumed was just another fan, but nothing could be farther from the truth. My eyes got bigger as I saw the guy pull a large black gun from his waistband. It was as if everything and everyone was moving in slow motion and nobody saw what was happening but me. My mouth was moving but the words were stuck in my throat. Breeze continued to smile as he walked towards me thinking it was him that was making me speechless, I tried to scream as the gunman raised his weapon to the back of Breeze's head but my warning never got the chance to be heard as the shot split his head in half and sent blood and brain fragments flying everywhere and everyone running and screaming. I never even felt Monica dragging me out of the park, it seemed as if I was still standing there watching Breeze's lifeless body take an eternity to hit the ground. But I wasn't standing there. I was back in the truck with Monica and the girls and we were on the highway. How we got there I don't know, but somebody had to shake me vigorously to snap me out of my trance.

"Girl snap out of it, pull yourself together are you okay?" I think it was Terri who asked.

"I saw the whole thing. I watched it happen, I saw who did it." I managed to mutter out.

Monica slapped me viciously across the face to snap me out of it.

"Hey, hey , hey. You aint see shit. Do you hear me? You aint see a motherfuckin' thing so get that thought out ya' head right the fuck now!"

RESCUE ME

I was awakened by a soft kiss on my lips. I thought I was dreaming so I didn't hop up right away. I was still trying to enjoy the dream of Travon and me making love again. But I was forced to open my eyes when I felt the kiss on my lips again.

"Rise and shine pretty." Travon said, as he stood over me.

"Hey, what are you doing here?" I asked; glad to see him but still half asleep.

"I heard there was a damsel in distress so I came running." He said, showing off his million-dollar smile.

"Captain Outlaw to the rescue huh?" I said, laughing.

"Well you know. I just make it do what it do." He replied, chuckling with me.

"Mmm Hmm. So what are you really doing here?" I asked, really wanting to know.

"Well I heard a little about what happened to you this morning, and I feel somewhat responsible. So I'm here to help." He responded, with the most sincere look on his face.

"Really? And just how do you plan on doing that?" I asked, sitting up.

"You just be ready by the time I get back, and I'll explain everything." He said, and then he kissed me on the forehead and walked out of the room. Monica quickly stuck her head in the room.

"You can thank me later." She said, grinning from ear to ear and dipping her head back out of the room. I just exhaled and flung myself back on the bed and thought to myself. "*What is going on?*"

THE REAL
MR. OUTLAW

TRAVON

I had received a text message from D-Boy, he spoke in our normal code and let me know that something was wrong. But I didn't know exactly what it was. So I proceeded to the meeting place with caution. When I got to the abandoned warehouse I scoured the area looking for anything that might have been out of place. Strange or suspicious people standing around, cars in the parking lot that I hadn't seen before or anything that was out of the ordinary. I checked, and double checked and everything seemed all good. So I proceeded to the front door, and gave the secret knock. After a few seconds D-Boy cautiously came to the door with his Glock 9mm in his hand.

"Okay Dee, what's the big emergency?" I asked, looking around once more before I walked into the building.

"Yo. Me and L.V. went to drop that package off and them B-More niggas tried to jack us." D-Boy explained, excited and angry.

"What? What the fuck are you talking about? I thought you said those B-More niggas was cool?" I asked, frustrated and unable to believe what I was hearing.

"Look man, they was cool. We been dealing with them for a minute now with no problem and then all of a sudden they flipped on us."

"Okay. You said they *tried* to jack you. So you got away with the stuff right?"

92   *Sean Wright*

"We got something even better than that. Follow me." D-Boy said, smiling and leading me through the hallways of the abandoned building.

"What can possibly be better than that?" I asked, really wanting to know.

"Take a look at this shit." He said, pulling a duffle bag from behind an old furnace and throwing it to me.

"Got damn. How much is in here?" I asked, shocked to see all the money that was in the bag.

"150 thousand nigga. A hundred and fifty fucking thousand." He answered, excitedly.

"Oh so you got away with the merchandise and them faggot niggas money? That's what's up." I said, congratulating him.

"But wait. There's more. Come on." He instructed. I followed him throughout the winding hallways of this building until we reached the bathroom where I was shocked to see L.V. standing over the bathtub with blood all over his shirt and a gun in his hand.

"Oh shit nigga are you hit?" I asked, rushing over to him.

"Nah. Never that. This blood belongs to this pussy right here." L.V. said, pointing into the tub. When I looked into the bathtub there was one of the stick up kids, tied up and badly beaten with duct tape over his mouth. He was really badly beaten. His face was bloody and looked like a piece of raw meat. And his eyes were damn near swollen shut. He kind of looked like Rocky at the end of part one.

"Is that nigga dead?" I asked.

"No but he wishes he was, he's just taking a little nap." L.V. said, jokingly.

"Wake that bitch up." I instructed.

"Okay boss, my pleasure." L.V. said. And in one swift motion, he pulled his gun from the shoulder hol-

A Gangster's Melody 93

ster and smacked the stick up kid across the face, sending blood splattering against the bathtub wall.

"Wake up motherfucker." I said, kneeling down whispering in his ear, and pulling my Desert Eagle. 40. Caliber from my waistband as he struggled to keep his eyes open. "Now I'm going to ask your bitch ass some questions, and you're going to respond by shaking your head yes or no. If there is a question that requires explaining, I will remove the tape and let you answer. However, if you scream, I will shoot you, if you try and call for help, I will shoot you, and last but not least, if you lie about anything, then we will all shoot you. Do you understand me motherfucker?" I asked him, as he nodded his head weakly and I cocked my gun.

"You can try and get him to talk, but I'm pretty sure I shattered his jaw." L.V. said, with a chuckle.

"Yeah. I only kept him alive because I knew you would want to have a few words with him." D-Boy said.

"Okay motherfucker. Do you know who I am?" I asked. He slowly shook his head no. "Of course you don't because nobody in their right mind would try and take anything from Travon Outlaw. How many of them was it?" I said, turning to D-Boy and L.V.

"It was him and two more, but them faggots bounced once we started letting off them shots, ya heard?" D-Boy stated, proudly.

"Yeah. I popped this bitch in the leg so he didn't get too far, but his boys left him." L.V. added.

"Okay. Today is your lucky day. I'm going to let your bitch ass live." I said, removing the duct tape.

"Oh my God. Thank you man. I swear I didn't know. And I still don't know who you are." The stick up kid said, weak yet excited about his new chance at life.

"Yeah I feel you. And that's why I'm going to let you live. But I need you to deliver a message to your people." I informed him.

"Okay dog anything. I'll do anything. What's the message?" He asked, happy about being set free.

"Let your boss know that fucking with Travon Outlaw just cost you an arm and a leg." I said, with a sinister smile on my face.

"I don't get it?" He replied, looking stupid.

"You're about to?" I said standing and raising my gun. I fired a shot into his arm, and then another into his leg. The 40. caliber bullets ripped through his flesh like a pellet gun through loose leaf paper. As I alternated between hitting the arm and the leg D-Boy and L.V. followed suit. We fired and mangled his limbs until there was almost nothing left. But I need him alive so I ordered a cease-fire.

"Drop this bitch ass nigga off on the main strip in his hood, and meet me back at the suite.Be careful. And if anybody out there even looks at you wrong you light they ass up. It's time to let these motherfuckers know how we get down." I stated coldly.

THE RESCUE

Just as he had promised. Travon came back to get me. I still had no idea what was going on, but I had no choice but to go with the flow, at least for right now. Besides, even if I wanted to go back to Mama Belle's which I didn't; she had made it abundantly clear that I could never go back there. Travon had finished loading the last of my things into his Porsche truck

"Okay pretty are you ready to roll?" Travon asked, getting into the car.

"I guess." I stated, nervously. Monica had stuck her head into the passenger side window and whispered into my ear.

"Damn bitch, you ain't been here but a hot minute and you done came up already. My only regret is that you didn't really get a chance to learn anything from me." Monica said, sounding disappointed.

"She'll be fine. She's in good hands." Travon replied, reassuring her.

"I'll call you later girl." I said, giving Monica a kiss on the cheek.

"You make sure you do. And what are you going to do about your grandmother?" she asked, motioning with her eyes at the fact that Mama Belle was on the porch watching the whole thing.

"I don't have a grandmother. I'll call you later. Let's go Tray." Travon pulled off and we drove for a few blocks in silence until I spoke up.

"Okay Travon, what's the deal? Where are we going and why did you have me bring all of my things?" I asked, curiously.

"Well it's like this. I know this is going to sound crazy because we just met, but I'm really feeling you. And I think I'm feeling you even more because you're not from here and you're not like these other chicks. You smart; intelligent, good looking and you're not impressed by my money." He replied, still driving never taking his eyes off the road.

"Look Travon, I appreciate the compliments and all but you haven't answered my questions. Where are we going?" I stated, really wanting to know.

"Well the way I see it, I'm going to be going back and forth from New York to Baltimore on business. So I'm buying a Condo in a very nice and expensive area. I'm hardly ever going to be there so I want you to stay there. All expenses paid, and I've even got a brand new Mercedes s600 that I don't use, you can have that to run around in." He stated.

"Travon I don't know what to say. This is all happening too fast." I replied, in a state of shock.

"Yeah, I know, but it's all good mommy. Look, you don't have a good, stable place to stay right now and I'm about to buy a crib that I'm never going to be at, so it'll be like you're house sitting for me."

"That's just it Travon. That'll be your shit that you can put me out of anytime you feel like it. Then I'll be right back to square one, and for all of that I might as well stay with my grandmother. Thanks but no thanks." I stated, adamantly.

"Look baby, I feel where you're coming from, but I don't get down like that. Best believe, if I give you something it's yours to keep."

"All of that sounds good, but you don't even know me."

"I don't have to know you baby, I know me and I know what I want."

"This is crazy."

"So. You ain't never did nothing crazy before?"

A Gangster's Melody 97

"Yeah, but not like this. I think I'm going to have to say no Tray." I replied, Travon was in shock and couldn't believe that I had just turned down such a generous offer.

"Okay. I'll tell you what. Just to prove to you how I get down, I will put it in your name." He stated.

"What did you say?" I replied, not believing what I was hearing.

"You heard me. Everything I buy for you I will put in your name. This way if you want to *you* can put *me* out." He replied, while laughing.

"Okay. Travon, one thing I hate is a liar. So don't try and bullshit me by telling me you're gonna buy this expensive crib and put it in my name. Just stop it. Cut the bullshit right now please." I stated, angrily. Travon just looked over at me and grabbed his cell phone. He put it on speaker phone and began to dial a number.

"What's your last name?" He asked.

"What?" I asked, wondering where he was going with this.

"Your last name ma. What's your last name?" he asked again, rushing me.

"Da- Davis. Why?" I stuttered before a voice came across the speaker phone signaling that someone had picked up the line.

"Elite Structures and Real Estate. This is Mike how can I help you?" The voice said.

"Hey Mike. It's Travon what's up?" Travon replied.

"Hey Mr. Outlaw. How's it going? All ready to take ownership of the new property?" Mike asked.

"Well that's what I was calling you about Mike."

"Mr. Outlaw you're not pulling out are you?" Mike asked, nervously.

"No Mike, relax your commission is safe. I just want to change the name on the paperwork from my name to a Ms. Tiffany Davis." Travon said, with a smile on his face.

"Well unfortunately Mr. Outlaw it's not that simple. There's the matter off Ms. Davis' credit history. We'll have to see if she qualifies and then.." Mike said before Travon cut him off.

"Hey mike listen, everything is still everything. I'm still fronting all the cash all we're doing today is changing the name on the paperwork. Now can you make that happen for me or do I have to take my business across the street to that other company with that fine ass receptionist?" Travon said, slightly raising his voice.

"Hold on Mr. Outlaw, that won't be necessary. I'm sure I can arrange things just the way you want them." Mike said, reassuringly.

"Yeah Okay. I knew you was the man. I'll bring Ms. Davis by later to sign the papers.

"Okay. Mr. Outlaw. I'll be here." Mike replied. Travon hung up the phone and grabbed me by the hand.

"Are you convinced that I'm real yet?" He asked.

"I can't believe you just did that." I said, in a total state of shock.

"Well it's real baby. We'll drop your stuff off at the hotel and then I'll take you by to see the place. You can stay at the suite for a few days until the condo is ready." I was overwhelmed.

"I don't know what to say." I responded.

"You don't have to say anything. Just be loyal and faithful." He replied.

"Faithful? Are you trying to tell me something Travon?" I asked, smiling.

"Baby I'm not trying to tell you something you don't already know. You done lucked up and got a good nigga your first night out. So just sit back and en-

A Gangster's Melody   99

joy the ride." He said, before leaning over and kissing me.

"Travon, I'm going to ride with you, but don't make me fuck you up when it's all said and done. I know you're in the music business and you got wall to wall groupies, so don't try to play me." I stated, firmly.

"Listen Tiffany. I 'm going to keep it real with you. I've been through the whole groupie thing when I was younger. But I'm older now and I'm looking for more. I mean, think about it. I could have picked any woman in that club last night, but I chose you." He stated before I burst out in laughter.

"What the hell is so funny?" he asked.

"Because you said that *you* chose *me*?"

"Yeah and?"

"Nigga how do you know I didn't choose you?"

"Because I'm a player that's why?" He responded, popping his collar.

"Whatever, just drive player. And stay away from that fine ass receptionist at that Real Estate office across the street that you were talking about." I said, playfully punching him in is arm.

"Oh baby, I ain't never been across the street. I was just spitting some of that good old New York game." Travon said, laughing.

THE BIG PAYBACK

HORSE

"Two rappers? Ya'll niggas couldn't handle two motherfucking rappers? What type of bullshit is that?" Horse screamed to the top of his lungs, while his soldiers stood there and took the verbal assault that they were being hit with.

"Horse man listen." Maleek started to explain but was abruptly cut off.

"Nah Fuck that. I heard enough. Ya'll just going to let theses niggas from up top come down here and take food out of your mouths? Out of your kids' mouths?" Huh?" Horse replied, still yelling.

"Horse you don't understand man. Them NY niggas is fucking ruthless. I mean we followed the plan just like you said, but it's like they were one step ahead of us the whole time. I'm telling you, them niggas is about their business man. Horse, when I say them niggas is on point, I mean them niggas is on..." Devin never got to finish his praising. Horse swiftly pulled his gun from his waistline and smacked Devin across the face sending him crashing to the floor.

"Shut your bitch ass up. Is-this-the-type-of –bitch-ass-soldiers I got working for me?" Horse stated while delivering powerful kicks to Devin's ribs and mid section.

"Well is it?" he asked looking around the room at the frightened faces.

"This nigga sucking them NY niggas dicks and shit. As a matter of fact, open your motherfucking mouth." He demanded, bending down.

Devin was apparently afraid for his life and refused to open his mouth.

"Oh you ain't gonna open up huh? Yo Rock, Sammy, give this pussy some assistance." Horse ordered.

It was then that Rock and Sammy stepped forward and each grabbed Devin by an arm and yanked him to his feet. Rock and Sammy were Horse's personal security. They both stood about 6'6 and weighed about 300 lbs of pure muscle. When they got him to his feet rock delivered a crushing blow to his kidney forcing Devin to open his mouth. Horse stepped up and shoved his gun in Devin's mouth knocking a few teeth out.

"Now since you sucking so much New York dick, suck on this. SUCK IT NIGGA. Or I'm going to put your brains on that back wall." Horse yelled, through gritted teeth.

Devin fearing for his life started sucking on the barrel of the gun. Some of the other soldiers are pointing and laughing, while others are shaking their heads in disbelief.

"Ya'll see this shit? Look at this faggot motherfucker. I don't need no gay ass soldiers in my army. Somebody cancel this bitch's contract." Horse said, throwing a wad of money on the floor. But before anybody can react Maleek steps forward and puts a bullet in Devin's head.

"Ooh, now that's gangster." Horse said, showing his approval.

"Damn baby. That was your older brother." Rock said, talking to Maleek.

"No nigga, That was business." Maleek stated, picking the money up off of the floor.

SETTLING IN

I had been with Travon for about a year now, and so far my life was just as beautiful as he promised it would be. I had cars, money, clothes, jewelry and most importantly three beauty salons that were doing exceptionally well. Travon made sure that I was always happy and that I never wanted for anything. He was becoming a very big figure in the music industry. D-Boy and The Realm Squad had sold over 3 million records and our lifestyle reflected the money that he made from managing them. There were a few downsides to living this life, I wish my parents were alive to see that I had made something of myself; they would both have been overjoyed at the fact that I accomplished my dreams of graduating from cosmetology school. My graduation was bitter sweet because as I crossed the stage and accepted my diploma, I looked out into the crowd and the two seats that my parents were supposed to occupy were filled with Travon and Monica, Terri and LaShawn were there too. I sent Mama Belle an invitation but she didn't show up. I didn't expect her to after the big fight that we had. I attempted to reach out to her just to see if she needed anything because I know my dad would have wanted it that way. But she never returned the three phone calls and messages I left for her, so that chapter of my life was officially closed. The other problem with living this lifestyle is that it gets lonely. Travon is always in and out of town and he asked me to cut back on hanging out with Monica and the girls because he said they had a bad reputation and that I was above their way of thinking, behaving, and living. In a way he was right, I never really agreed with the life that the Stiletto Divas led, I was just trying to fit in. but when this overnight success kicked in I realized that the lifestyle that they lead is not for me, and my parents would be very disappointed in me if I chose that route. I mean, don't get me wrong. I didn't completely distance myself from them, but at the request of my man and future husband I did cut back on the hanging out and wild activities. Travon was now a very prominent figure in the music industry and I would do nothing to damage his great reputation or create a bad one for myself. I was truly in love with Travon, and I couldn't wait to become Mrs. Outlaw and carry his child. But his busy lifestyle was making me lonely and I had to call him and let him know. I picked up my Blackberry and dialed his cell number.

"Hey what's up baby? When are you coming home?" I asked, in my sweetest baby girl voice.

"Come on baby. You already know how this part of the game goes. This music and traveling is what keeps you living the way you like to live and doing the things you like to do. Come on Tiffany it's been almost a year, you should be well adjusted by now." Travon responded.

"I know. But I'm lonely Tray." I fired back, in an even more whiney voice.

"Lonely? With all that money I left there? Go buy yourself some friends." He responded, laughing.

"Shut up Tray. I'm serious. Now come on. You don't like me hanging around Monica and them no more, so I cut back on hanging out with them. But I'm always here by myself in this big ass house. How come I can't never go with you to New York?" I responded.

"Tiffany, you've been up here with me a few times so what are you talking about?" he responded, sounding a little agitated.

A Gangster's Melody 105

"Yeah Tray, but when I do come what do I do besides sit at the hotel, or go shopping and occasionally go to your apartment or the studio?"

"Okay baby listen. I know it gets a little lonely from time to time, but I'll be home soon I promise. Now look, I got to go. Keep it tight and I'll holler at you later."

"Okay Tray but you better call me."

"I will baby." He answered before hanging up. I just deep sighed and plopped down on the bed. I would have to call the girls and do some shopping to make me feel better.

LOOSEN UP

"Damn son I never thought I'd see the day when you would lose your pimp card going soft on a bitch. What the fuck has gotten into you with all of this lovey dovey shit?" D-Boy said as Travon hung up the phone.

"Let it go Dee." Travon instructed, not in the mood to be ridiculed.

"Nah son. I been watching you for the longest and you really head over heels for this bitch." D-Boy continued, with the antagonizing.

"Look Dee, I'm going to tell you one more time to let the shit go. Why are you hating anyway? Just because I found myself somebody who is more than a groupie or a fuck buddy? Somebody who got a little interest in and who ain't taking me for all my paper like them bitches you fuck with?" Travon barked back.

"Whatever nigga. You got the nerve to talk, you done gave the bitch a crib, a whip and God knows how much paper. And the real bullshit is I'm the one who put the bullshit in her drink that night and your cock blockin ass end up beating it." D-Boy fired back.

"What did you say?" Travon asked, making sure that he heard correctly.

"That night of the after party. I slipped the bullshit in her drink so I could tear that ass up. But you bitched up and did the cock blocking shit. I'll admit you was right. She was a tough nut to crack until I ended up putting the shit in her drink." D-Boy said, with a smile on his face.

"You stupid motherfucker. Do you know she blamed me for taking advantage of her, and for taking her fucking virginity?" Travon said, now screaming to the top of his lungs.

A Gangster's Melody 107

"Oh shit. That bitch was a virgin? Aww nigga you should be thanking me instead of being mad at me. So tell me, does she suck a good dick?" D-Boy said, laughing loudly, before Travon punched him in the face and knocked him to the floor as they simultaneously pull their guns out.

"Nigga are we about to dance over a bitch?" D-boy asked, still in shock from the punch.

"Nah nigga. If we dance it's because you don't know when or how to shut the fuck up. Now put the hammer away and let's get back to business." Travon said, slowly lowering his weapon.

"You sucker for love ass nigga." D-Boy said, jokingly as Travon helps him up off the floor.

"Fuck you, you fucking hater." Travon responded, laughing.

TWO WORLDS COLLIDE

"Got damn look at them bitches." Maleek stated, as he pulled up next to Tiffany and the sat the light.

"Yeah all them bitches look good." Hydro agreed.

"Yeah but the driver is off the fucking chain." Maleek responded, blowing the horn and leaning over Hydro. "Excuse me pretty, how are you doing today?" Maleek asked Tiffany.

"I'm fine thank you." Tiffany responded, just being polite.

"Well in that case, why don't you and your friends follow me and my boys to get something to eat?" Maleek asked, not letting up.

"No. I'm sorry I can't. But thanks for the offer." Tiffany responded.

"Look baby. She don't speak for all of us. Just because Ms. Travon Outlaw is on lockdown, that ain't got shit to do with the rest of us." Terri said, leaning out of the window. The light turned green and Tiffany pulled off while Maleek just sat there holding up traffic.

"Yo. What are you doing? Drive nigga." Hydro said.

"Did you hear what that bitch just said?" Maleek asked, pulling off but making sure he kept Tiffany's truck in sight.

"Yeah motherfucker the bitch said she ain't going nowhere with you." Hydro joked

"No jackass. The bitch in the back called the driver Mrs.Travon Outlaw." Maleek stated.

"Yeah. So what?" Hydro answered confused.

"Travon Outlaw is the nigga that hit Jimmy up after we tried to jack his people." Maleek said, pulling out his cell phone.

A Gangster's Melody　　　　　　　　　　109

"Yo Horse what's up? It's Maleek. Yeah listen, that nigga Travon Outlaw? I'm sitting on his bitch right now. I say we snatch the bitch up and make that faggot nigga come see us."

"Nah chill. I want the nigga to sleep a little while longer. If we move now, he'll know that we are on to him." Horse replied.

"Yo Horse man. This motherfucker crippled my man Jimmy and he cost my brother Devin his life. Now how much longer are you going to let these niggas from up top run wild in your backyard?" Maleek barked, forgetting who he was talking to.

"Nigga hold the fuck up. Has something changed over the past couple of minutes? Did our roles reverse motherfucker? Nigga you work for me, I don't work for you. Now do what the fuck I say, and stop questioning me." Horse yelled into the phone before hanging up and causing Maleek to throw the phone down in anger.

"What did he say?" Hydro asked.

"Man he talking about let the shit ride out a little bit longer before we do anything."

Maleek answered, angrily while still switching lanes and following the girls.

"Yo man what are you doing? Horse said let that shit be." Hydro reminded him.

"Don't worry, I ain't going to pull the bitch coat to who we are, but I have to get this shit off of my chest." Maleek responded.

"Nigga you're going to get us killed" Hydro said, shaking his head as Maleek followed Tiffany into the bank parking lot. He parked a few feet away so that he wouldn't be noticed.

"Girl why are you going in? Why can't you just go to the ATM machine?" Monica asked Tiffany.

110 *Sean Wright*

"Because the ATM won't give you 10 gee's that's why." Tiffany replied.

"Oh Shit. Excuse me baller." Terri said jokingly.

"Aww girl shut up. It ain't even like that. Travon asked me to run a couple of errands for him until he gets back tomorrow." Tiffany replied. Before exiting the car and heading inside of the bank.

"Yeah bitch, run in there and get me my money." Maleek said, out loud but talking to himself.

"Come on dog. She could be in there getting 20 fucking dollars yo." Hydro urged.

"See man, that's why Horse don't promote your ass. Because you ain't a thinker. If she was going to get some chump change she would have gone to the ATM machine and not inside of the bank." Maleek stated.

"Maybe she lost her ATM card." Hydro said, dumbly.

"Nigga shut up and get ready. Here she comes." Maleek said, taking out his gun and drove over to block Tiffany's car in.

"Nigga what the hell are you doing? Didn't I tell you we ain't fucking with ya'll?" Tiffany snapped.

"Yeah bitch you said that. But you know us Baltimore cats is hard of hearing. Now where is it?" Maleek said, getting out of the car with his gun drawn.

"What are you talking about? I made a deposit to pay my light bill." Tiffany lied.

"Light bill huh? Okay I'll tell you what. If I search you and I don't find anything than I'll apologize and give you $1000 dollars for the inconvenience. However, if I find anything more than what I think a young lady usually travels with I'm going to put a hole in that pretty little face of yours. And then of course you know your friends are all going to get makeovers too. Now do you want me to check or are you going to come clean?" Maleek said before Tiffany reached into her

A Gangster's Melody

pocketbook and removed the envelope containing the ten thousand dollars and gave it to him.

"Jackpot." Maleek yelled, after looking inside the envelope. He was so excited that he never saw Monica stick a gun out of the window.

"Why don't you be a gentleman and give the lady her bread back?" Monica said, cocking the hammer on her snub nose .32.

"Very impressive, however you might want to focus your attention on my man in the car with me." Maleek stated, pointing to Hydro who had his two guns trained on Tiffany's truck.

"Now unless ya'll want to get Swiss cheesed the fuck up, I suggest you hand over the hammer, take this loss on the chin and roll out." Maleek demanded, taking Monica's gun and putting it in his waistband. "See shorty. Not letting me take you out just cost you an arm and a leg. Your man ought to find that funny." Maleek, stated as Hydro rolled his eyes at the fact that Maleek was dropping hints. Maleek then walked backwards to his car, got in and drove off laughing.

"Motherfucker. Travon is going to go through the fucking roof." Tiffany yelled.

LET THE
WOLVES LOOSE

"Okay baby calm down. I'll be there first thing in the morning. Don't worry. I'll take care of it. Fuck the money, there's plenty more where that came from. I'm just glad you're okay." Travon spoke into the telephone.

"Travon I'm scared to death. Can't you come home tonight?" Tiffany cried.

"Baby I'm in the middle of a very important project. But I swear I will leave first thing in the morning and get there before you even wake up." Travon responded.

"Baby you know I never try and come between you and your business, but you have to understand, I ain't never had no gun put to my head before. And for my own personal reasons I'm terrified of them. And I can still hear that motherfucker laughing and talking about me not going out with him would cost me an arm and a leg and you would find that funny. I can't believe.." Tiffany explained, before being cut off.

"Back up. What did he say about an arm and a leg?" Travon asked.

"He was just talking shit that's all" Tiffany said.

"Look baby. I'm going to put this project on hold and I'll be home in a few hours."

"Thank you baby."

"No problem ma."

"Travon?"

"Yeah?"

"I love you."

"I love you too baby." Travon said, before hanging up the phone and turning to D-Boy, L.V. and a few more of his goons.

A Gangster's Melody   113

"Alright, ya'll niggas strap up and let's ride out. Them B-More niggas is definitely out of pocket. They put the burner to Tiffany's head and snatched ten stacks from her." Travon instructed.

"Damn, them niggas just don't learn do they?" L.V. responded

"D-Boy, I want you to call whatever loyal goons we got down there and get a line on those pussies." Travon ordered.

"I'm on it." D-Boy said, dialing numbers on his cell phone.

"Enough of this laying low shit. It's time to mash on these motherfuckers New York style." Travon said.

The whole ride back to B-More all I could do was think of how to make them pussy's pay for what they did. I had tried to chill and move in silence like bad boys do, but they pushed my buttons, now there was no turning back. It was time to take the gloves off and make an example out of everyone who was involved. My father once told me your name is all you have, and my mother followed that with, your name will get you farther in life than money will. And with that being said…there was blood to be shed.

When I got home Tiffany was sitting in the living room waiting for me. As soon as I walked in she ran and grabbed me hugging me and crying uncontrollably.

"Okay ma. It's all right. I'm home now ain't nothing to worry about." I assured her

"Baby thank you for coming home." She said, still not letting go.

"It's nothing baby. Don't worry about it. Now go on up to bed and I'll be there in a minute." I said, kissing her on the forehead.

"Okay baby." She said, wiping her tears and heading upstairs. I was on my way to the kitchen to fix my-

114　　　　　　　　　　　　　　　　　*Sean Wright*

self a drink when I got a call from D-Boy on my cell phone.

"Tell me something good fam." I said, as I poured my drink

"Yeah, I got a line on them B-More cats." He responded.

"Got damn that was fast."

"Will you'll be surprised what a little money and a whole lot of gun play will get you these days."

"Okay that's what's up. I want you to give the info to Lorenzo, Big John and Skillz and have them pick me up in the morning so we can handle this shit." I instructed.

"Lorenzo and Big John? Why not let me and L.V. handle this shit like we always do?"

"Because ya'll niggas is on every major video channel and have a few hit records under your belt and everyone knows ya'll already, including them stick up kids. So as much as I would love for ya'll to handle this for me I need fresh faces on this one." I explained.

"A'ight man I feel you. I'll send Lorenzo and them by to get you in the morning."

"What I do want you to do is sit on the crib for me tomorrow and make sure Tiffany is alright."

"I got you. You need somebody over there tonight?"

"Nah, I'm cool. A motherfucker come up in here tonight, he done made a bad decision." I said, tapping both guns in my waist.

"Alright, I'll see you in a few hours. Call me if you need me."

"You already know." I said, before I hung up.

The next day Lorenzo, Big John, and Skillz picked me up just as I ordered. These were three of the best soldiers I had that didn't actually come from New York, but if I didn't tell you they weren't New Yorkers you wouldn't be able to tell. Everything from the

A Gangster's Melody

115

clothes to the slang to the swagger screamed out New York. When they picked me up, the mission was to head over to a stash house that they had gotten a tip on. We pulled up across the street from the house to do a little reconnaissance and I was shocked to see what I saw.

"There's the crib right there. Everything in there belongs to a heavy player out of North West D.C. who calls himself Horse. The word is that his boys are the ones that tried to jack D-Boy and L.V. and ran up on Tiffany. Strangely enough though, the security is minimal. You got those two young boys right there on the steps. Now I'm sure the little niggas is holding heat but they young and inexperienced. Instead of watching the house they be watching the bitches walk back and forth. Now once you get inside you got one armed guard and a bunch of naked bitches cooking, bagging, and counting money." Skillz reported.

"It sounds too easy. How reliable is your information." I asked, not believing my eyes or ears.

"Very reliable boss. I'm fucking three of the bitches that work in there and they all say the exact same thing." Skillz reassured.

"You fucking three of them bitches son?" Lorenzo asked.

"Hell yeah, and neither one of them know about the other ones." Skillz said, bragging.

"Okay you big pimp you." Lorenzo said, giving him dap.

"Alright, enough of the fucking player of the year nominations. Let's get back to business. Here's the plan. We get three of the baddest bitches we know. We'll have two of them distract the young boys, and take them around the corner, where we'll have somebody waiting to hold them down. The third bitch will walk up to the front door and let the dumb motherfucker inside know his boys are getting mashed on. When he runs out of the house, we'll force him back in and take them for everything they got. However. Skillz if you're wrong about this you gonna have hell to pay. You feel me?" I stated, firmly.

"Nah dog, trust me it's all good. I'm telling you, all them bitches told me the same thing." Skillz said, trying to reassure me.

"Alright, in that case I want this shit to go down as soon as it gets dark. Where can we find some thorough bitches at?" I asked.

"How about them scandalous ass Stiletto Diva chicks that Tiffany fuck with?" Big John asked.

"Nah nigga, they thorough as fuck but you know I can't have Tiffany knowing what I do."

"Okay. I can get Candace, Felicia, and Patrice to handle it. They put in work for me before so I know they can hold this down. But they don't come cheap." Lorenzo informed me.

"I don't give a fuck what them hoes cost. Make the call and let's get this shit done." I instructed, before tapping Big John on the shoulder. "Let's go." I instructed, and we pulled off.

THE OLIVE BRANCH

After what happened to me at the bank Travon was staying home a lot more often. And coincidentally I hadn't had a problem since. I never even saw that guy again. I hadn't really chilled with Monica in a while so I decided to stop by and see her. Every once in a while we would do girls night out or just chill at her crib. But tonight we just enjoyed the weather and sat on her porch and kicked it like little schoolgirls.

"So what's been up girl? You done got all big time and don't fuck with your bitches no more huh?" Monica said, playfully punching me in my arm.

"I'm good. And you know it ain't even like that." I said, defending myself.

"Bitch I can't tell. I mean we talk on the phone and shit but you don't really come through no more. That nigga got you on lock" She said, teasing me.

"No he don't have me on lock. But we are in love and I can't be out there doing Stiletto Diva shit. I wouldn't even play my baby like that. And besides there's no need to. Isn't the SD mission statement to get hooked up with a baller? Well that's what I did." I stated proudly.

"Yeah bitch, but you fell in love with the mark" she replied, as we both shared a laugh.

"Whatever, anyway what's been up?" I asked.

"Girl it's the same shit. Getting this bread from these stupid ass niggas. Can you believe I got proposed to three times this week?" She said laughing.

"Okay pimpstress. Some things never change." I said, jokingly.

"Yeah well somebody gotta hold it down. Ya'll bitches is tripping. Terri stupid ass done went and started devoting all her time to one nigga too. I mean he got bread, And great credit but he's a fucking loser in every other sense of the word. And she just be taking him for what little he do got. He ain't even no major player. She met him at the gotdamn grocery store. And Lashawn done lowered her standards too. Instead of finding new marks she just keep recycling the old ones.

"Wow that's crazy." I said.

"Yeah well, enough about those simple bitches. What's up with you? I see you got another brand new whip. What's that, the new Benz?" Monica asked looking passed me.

"Yeah it's the new 600 Coupe Limited Edition. Travon got it for me last week." I stated proudly.

"That's what's up girl I'm proud of you. So let me ask you something. You ain't never spoke to Ms. Lula Belle again since ya'll had that fight?" Monica asked me.

"Nope. I don't have nothing to say to her. I mean, even after all that shit went down I sent her some money on three different occasions just because I had it like that. And she cashed the checks but never called to say thank you not even once. So fuck her she is dead to me now." I snapped.

"Well I happen to know she is very much alive because I saw her get into an ambulance earlier. I called you and left you a message about it." She said.

"Really? So what's up for your birthday? I asked, not really caring about her previous comment.

"Well you know we gonna do it up real big at the club, no doubt about that. But for real though, you need to check up on your grandmother." She said.

"Come on Moe. Don't start that shit. I told her after that night that I was done with her. The way she disrespected my parents, especially my mother. Fuck

A Gangster's Melody 119

what she said about me. But I ain't letting that other shit ride. The bitch spent my money then didn't even say thank you. For all I care she can drop dead." I barked, feeling myself getting emotional as Mama Belle's car pulled up. Mr. Rufus was driving and he came around to her door to help her out. As she made her way up the walk way she shot me a cold and sinister stare then rolled her eyes and continued on into her house. I returned the rolling of the eyes and continued my conversation.

"Anyway, like I was saying we're going to get it popping for your birthday. Make sure ya'll bring ya'll nappy headed asses down to the Salon so I can twist ya'll up on the house." I said.

"Damn bitch it's about time you gave us something on the house. You got the hottest hair joint in the city for the past 5 months and you just now giving something up for free?" Monica joked.

"Oh bitch shut up. I learned how to hustle from you. So kick yourself in the ass" I joked back.

"Nah seriously Tiffany, I'm proud of you. The house, the cars, the degree, the salons. Keep doing your thing girl. And hold on to that nigga Travon, I talk a lot of shit but he is definitely holding you down so don't mess that up. And by the way tell him I want front row and backstage passes to the Jay Z and Mary J. Blige concert for my birthday. And tell him to tell Jay Z to shout me out for my birthday." She requested.

"I got you, but speaking of Travon, let me go girl I'll holler at you later." I said, standing up and kissing her on the cheek

"Look at you rushing home to that nigga. He got you dick whipped really good." She said, laughing.

"Yeah whatever, it ain't even like that. It's just that this music shit got him running in and out of town all crazy. So I have to get my time in when I can." I explained.

"Call it what you want. Your ass is whooped." She replied.

"Anyway. I'll call you later." I said, heading towards my car.

"Hey. On some real shit you need to squash that shit with Ms. Belle." She said

"Good bye Monica." I said, not looking back, and she was right. I was rushing home to my man. And yes he did have me whipped.

JACK MOVE

"Damn, them young boys still out there?" Don't they switch up shifts or anything? Travon asked, as they were once again parked across the street from Horse's stash house.

That's what I'm trying to tell you. They real sloppy with they shit." Skillz replied.

"Easy money baby." Lorenzo added.

It better be easy money because bullets is expensive and I'd hate to have to waste both clips on them motherfuckers in there." Big John said, semi-jokingly.

"Okay killer, calm down. Everything's going to go down nice and smooth, ain't it Skillz?" Travon asked, for reassurance.

"That's right boss." Skill reassured.

"Alright Renzo, is everybody in place?" Travon asked.

"Yeah, the goons are around that corner and the bitches are around the other corner. Everybody is waiting for the call." Lorenzo pointed out.

"Look at them boys all off point and shit. It's a whole new world down here. Well anyway, time to take them to school. Renzo, make the call. Let's get this show on the road." Travon instructed."

"I'm on it boss, but are you sure you want to go in with us? I mean, that's what you pay us for. So we can get our hands dirty and you can stay clean. You know, the pawns protect the king." Lorenzo stated, loyally.

"Listen dog, I feel you on that. But in every good war movie the general goes to war with his soldiers. So let's do it." Travon said, cocking both of his weapons.

"Damn, that's what's up. That's why I fucking love you dog. I would take a fucking case or a bullet for you

A Gangster's Melody   123

any day. Just remember that." Lorenzo stated, whole-heartedly as he chirped the waiting parties.

"Everybody ready?" He asked

"Yeah we ready." Felicia answered.

"Ready over here too" Gary chirped in.

"Alright, Felicia go, Gary you stand by. And Felicia, make it good." Lorenzo instructed.

"Don't I always make it good baby?" Felicia flirted.

Felicia and Candace head down the street walking and looking as sexy and provocative as possible. Felicia stood about 5 foot 6 with a pretty dark chocolate skin tone. She wore her hair cut in a Rhianna-like style. Her body was stacked, measuring 38-24-40. She wore a pair of very short Dolce and Gabbana shorts and a form fitting half shirt. Candace on the other hand, was 5 foot 4 with a redbone complexion, and fire red hair that came down to the middle of her back. She wore Gucci sneakers and a one piece BCBG short set. She was just as stacked as Felicia was. Getting the show started, they walk passed the two young boys and started a conversation that they were sure would get their attention.

"Girl I sucked that niggas dick until he came all over my face and titties." Felicia said, loud enough for the young boys to hear.

"Was that before or after he was fucking you while you was sucking my clit?" Candace played along.

"Girl I don't even remember. There was so much fucking and sucking going on last night that my head was spinning." Felicia continued, noticing that the plan worked like a charm. She looked at one of them and licked her lips and he took the bait.

"Damn ladies, what's popping?" Young buck #1 asked.

"Please baby. Ya'll little niggas wouldn't know what to do with all of this." Candace responded, rubbing her ass provocatively.

"Shit baby are you crazy? Don't let the age fool you. We holds it down, and we got a pocket full of money." Young buck #2 stated, as he pulled a wad of money from his pocket.

"Sure you do little man. Come on girl let's go, here take the keys." Felicia said, tossing the keys to Candace who missed them on purpose so that she could bend over in front of the young boys and show that she wore no panties under her mini skirt.

"Hold on. Why ya'll leaving? We got the drink and we got the smoke. We about to get lit right here. Why don't ya'll chill with us?" Young buck #1 asked.

"Look boo. We are classy bitches. We don't stand on nobody's block and get smoked out. We do that in the comfort of our own homes. Now if ya'll think ya'll can hang, then come on and chill with us for a little while so we can turn ya'll young asses out." Felicia said, licking her lips again.

"Yeah ya'll kind of cute, so come on we'll play with you for a little while." Candace added, stroking young buck #1's cheek.

"Come on baby, can't we chill right here? We can't move from in front of this house right now." Young buck #1 pleaded.

"Aww shit ya'll little niggas can't even leave from in front of the crib? Come on girl let's get the fuck out of here." Candace said, grabbing Felicia's arm.

"Hold on. We just handling a little business right now but let's exchange numbers and we'll hook up later." Young buck # 2 said, trying to save face.

"Well walk us around the corner to our car at least damn. You can do that can't you?" Felicia asked, getting aggravated.

"Alright ma. But make it quick." Young buck # 2 said.

"Don't worry we will." Candace stated, slyly.

A Gangster's Melody 125

They walked around the corner side by side while Travon and the boys watched it finally go down from across the street.

"Alright Gary, ya'll are up." Lorenzo said, chirping the phone.

When they turned the corner Gary and his boys are pretending to shoot dice. When the girls and the young bucks walk passed, Gary and his boys pull their weapons and catch the young bucks off guard.

"Alright give it up young boys." Gary instructed, before chirping Lorenzo "We good over here."

"Alright cool. Patrice go." Lorenzo chirped.

Patrice made her way up to the front door and started banging with all of her might. Maleek looked through the peephole and then opened the door.

"Bitch what the fuck is wrong with you? Are you trying to get your pretty ass shot?" Maleek asked, not noticing that the two young bucks were missing.

"Yo. The young boys is getting jacked up the block. They told me to come and get you." Patrice said, frantically as if she were trying to receive an Oscar for her performance.

"What the fuck? Which way?" Maleek said, looking around.

"Down there and around the corner." Patrice said, pointing to the corner.

Maleek pulled out his gun and stepped passed Patrice. As soon as she was behind him she pulled out her gun and put it to the back of his head, and signaled for Travon and the boys to come across the street.

"Drop it pussy." Patrice instructed.

"Bitch are you trying to die?" Maleek asked, still not dropping his weapon.

"Nah nigga is you?" Patrice asked, cocking the hammer.

126   *Sean Wright*

At the sight of Travon and the boys coming across the street with their guns drawn Maleek finally dropped his weapon on the ground.

"Let's go playboy, back inside." Travon ordered.

"Are ya'll motherfuckers crazy? Do you know who shit ya'll fucking with?" Maleek barked.

"Shut the fuck up and open the door." Big John said, hitting Maleek in the back of the head with his gun.

Maleek reluctantly opened the door and just as Lorenzo said there are women totally naked at the table bagging drugs, cooking drugs and counting money. All are naked except for one who is wearing an apron. They pushed Maleek through the door and caught the ladies by surprise.

"All ya'll bitches get your hands up and shut the fuck up." Travon demanded.

"Yo Skillz watch the door, Big John watch this motherfucker." Lorenzo instructed.

"Bags." Travon yelled out, and they all pulled out garbage bags from their back pocket.

"Okay ladies let's go. Everything in the bag. Every pack, capsule, dollar and every grain of fucking coke. Travon ordered, waiving his gun, as the girls did what they were told.

"Ya'll clowns just signed your own death certificates. Do you know whose shit ya'll are fucking with?" Maleek said.

"Keep it up pussy, and your next words will be your last ones." Big John said, cocking his gun and putting it to his head.

"Look motherfucker you tell that nigga Horse that we tried to play fair. All I wanted was a piece of the pie, now I'm taking the whole fuckin' thing." Travon said.

A Gangster's Melody 127

"Yeah ya'll bitch ass niggas think it's a fucking game? Tell your boss the game is over." Lorenzo said, momentarily taking his eyes off of the girls.

That split second caused all hell to break loose. The girl with the apron pulls out an Ak-47. Her first target is Lorenzo, and she catches him in the shoulder. The other girls flip the table over and pull out guns that are duct taped under the table. Travon and the guys take cover and return fire. Maleek tries to run, but doesn't get far before Big John shoots him in the leg. The gun battle doesn't last long because except for the table the girls have no real cover. While Travon, and the boys have the walls, and different sections of the house for perfect cover. It isn't long before each of the girls is picked off one at a time. Except for the one with the apron who is laying down heavy fire with the AK-47. So far she has hit Lorenzo in the shoulder and Big John in the leg. The barrage of bullets coming from her weapon is so steady that the guys can't come from behind their cover to return fire. The girl gets smart and starts to shoot through the walls to draw them out into the open. But just when her plan was starting to work, Gary who had snuck around to the side of the house, sticks his 9mm through the window and ends the assault with two well placed shots to the back of her head.

"Sounded like ya'll niggas needed some help." Gary said, jokingly looking through the window.

"You are always right on time son. Remind me to give you a bonus. Is everybody alright?" Travon asked, checking on his crew.

"Yeah I'm good, the bullet went stra'ight through. That fucking bitch got the drop on me." Lorenzo stated, grimacing in pain.

"Yeah and I'm going to tell the whole crew that you let a broad get the drop on you too." Big John joked.

"Yeah whatever. You should have seen your big fat ass trying to scurry across the living room when she popped you in the leg." Lorenzo joked back.

"Okay. Ya'll grab the shit and let's go." Travon ordered.

"What about him?" Skillz asked, pointing to Maleek.

"Oh yes my little messenger. I want you to tell your boy Horse that Travon Outlaw is in town and I'm going to make my presence felt until he can't take it no fucking more." Travon said, through gritted teeth.

"Travon Outlaw? You're Travon Outlaw?" Maleek said, grimacing and holding his leg.

"Yeah why? My name is starting to ring bells around here ain't it?" Travon joked.

"Yeah motherfucker. You and your bitch bought the rims for my truck. Thanks for the 10 gee's. I should have popped your bitch right after I took it, but I'd rather fuck her after my mans and them deal with your bitch ass." Maleek said, laughing. Those were his last words before Travon stood up and fired three shots into his face.

"Damn Tray? Now how are we going to get the message to Horse?" Skillz asked.

"Don't worry he'll get the message. Let's go." Travon ordered.

POLICE ON ALERT

"Will you look at this fucking shit?" Detective Johnson said, surveying the brutal crime scene.

"Yeah whoever came through here wasn't fucking around." His partner Detective Williams responded.

"Okay so let's piece this shit together." Detective Williams said, looking around.

"Okay, from what I can see a gun battle took place between the broads behind the table and whoever stood right about here." Detective Johnson said, pointing to the staircase where Travon stood about 2 hours ago.

"And right about here, and over there and over there." Detective Williams added, pointing to where Skillz, Big John, and Lorenzo each stood.

"Okay. Question? The line of fire is this way correct?" Detective Johnson asked pointing towards the door.

"Yup." Detective Williams concurred.

"Well then why is the back of this woman's head blown off? Let's see here, come on baby talk to me." Detective Johnson said, as he pulled out a flashlight and looked for clues.

"This motherfucker done went crazy, talking to dead naked women." Williams joked.

"Yeah I get practice every night when I go to bed with my wife." Johnson joked back.

"Now you know I'm going to tell her at the BBQ Saturday right?"

"I bet you will you snitch, Bingo." Johnson said, looking out of the window.

"What you got?" Williams asked.

"Another shooter took her out from right here. Must have snuck around back." Johnson said.

"Okay one mystery down. Next question. Who's this guy, one of the shooters?" Williams said, referring to Maleek.

"No it doesn't make sense."

"You're right. These are close range wounds. If they are close enough to take him out no need to be behind the table." "Well let's see who he was. At least he's got clothes on for us to go through." Johnson said, bending down and going through Maleek's pockets. "Maleek Stapelton. Ring a bell?" he asked his partner.

"No but my snitch knows everybody, hold on a second." He responded , As he dials a number on his cell phone.

"Hey what's up? ...Maleek Stapelton, give me the run down on him. Mmm hmm..Right right Okay. I owe you one. Talk to you later. Okay. Homeboy right here was the security for the ladies. This was apparently a stash house for a major player named Horse and according to my C.I. there's always two more guards outside of the house. So either their bodies will turn up or they were in on it." Williams stated.

"Okay. Last mystery. What do you make of that?" Johnson said, pointing to the bloody 718 on the wall.

"You got me on that one. I'll run it through the data base downtown and see if it's a new gang or something." Williams responded, before being interrupted by Lt. Daniels their superior officer.

"Sweet Jesus. Please tell me you guys have answers for me." Lt. Daniels pleaded.

"Pretty much a drug jack move sir. We've pretty much figured everything out except for the numbers on the wall." Williams answered.

"718 huh? Code name for any of the local gangs?" Lt. Daniels asked.

"None that we know of sir but we're going to run it through the system." Johnson answered.

A Gangster's Melody   131

"Well whatever you're going to do, do it fast. I want this mess cleared up A.S.A.P. I can already tell it's going to be raining bodies for the next few days." Lt. Daniels said.

BEAUTY AND THE BEATDOWN

I was at the shop doing Terry's hair for Monica's Birthday party later on that night. While doing Terry's hair she decided to fill Lashawn, Monica and myself in on her latest male victim.

"Yo. Did I tell ya'll that the nigga Gerard is trippin because he just got his credit card bill back?" Terry asked, nonchalantly as I flat ironed her hair.

"Well bitch he should spaz on you. You spent like $7500 dollars. You lucky he ain't two piece ya ass." Lashawn responded, matter of factly.

"Spaz for what? He gave me the credit card in the first place." Terry responded.

"Yeah but he told you to pay your cable bill. Bitch you re-decorated your entire living room." Monica jumped in.

"Damn, you are playing a dangerous game Terry." I chimed in.

"Look, it ain't my fault that his nose is wide open and he neglects his wife and kids just so I can get whatever I want. And the crazy thing is we ain't even fuck yet. All I let him do is eat the pussy. And for that, I get all my bills paid and his wallet is open whenever I want it." Terry replied.

"Oh shit, I forgot that nigga Gerard was married. Bitch you're a fucking home wrecker." Lashawn answered back.

"Look. The way I see it is, if a nigga ends up in my bed his home is already wrecked. I didn't put a gun to his head and ask him to trick all of his bread on me. Besides, as long as I'm taken care of what the fuck do I care about his wife and kids? Shit. That bitch better

A Gangster's Melody

charge it to the game. Fuck around and I'll be the next Mrs. Gerard McMillan." Terry stated, a little bit more hype this time.

It was just then that the woman under the hair dryer directly across from Terry sprung into action.

"Bitch is you fucking my husband?" She screamed, as she ran across the floor in Terry's direction in a fit of rage.

Unfortunate for her, that she never reached her destination. Monica had stepped in front of her, snatched her by her quick weave and initiated the assault that would ruin this poor girls night.

"Bitch is you trying to run up on my girl? Have you lost ya fucking mind?" Monica asked, before slapping the girl repeatedly across the face.

But the woman never had a chance to respond because Lashawn was next to spring into action. She grabbed the woman by the shirt and continuously began punching her in the face. Terry jumped out of the chair next.

"Hold that bitch still." She instructed, as Monica and Lashawn each grabbed an arm.

Terry rummaged through my top drawer until she found a stra'ight razor. She then headed over to where Monica and Lashawn had the girl held captive.

"Now bitch, you should have known better than to try and do some dumb shit like running up on me. If you had done your homework, you would have known right away that I am the wrong bitch to fuck with. Now I'm going to give you a constant reminder of who the fuck I am." Terry said, before grabbing the girl by her face and slowly but painfully carving a letter "T" in her cheek.

The girl screamed to the top of her lungs as I, along with my other customers just watched in horror and shock.

The way the girl grabbed her face and the blood squirted through her fingers, reminded me of a scene out of the worst horror movie you could imagine. Terry spat in the girls face, punched her in it, and then ordered her to leave the shop. Now it was my turn to spaz out as the rest of the girls celebrated their victory.

"A 'yo what the fuck is wrong with ya'll? This is my shop and my place of business. Look at all of this blood; look at all of this mess. The police are going to come and shut my shit down. I can't believe ya'll." I screamed hysterically.

"Yo Tiffany, calm that shit down. That bitch needed to get dealt with. She was out of pocket and you fucking know it. Now I'm sorry that shit had to get funky in your place of business. But when shit like that hits the fan, there ain't no right or wrong time to deal with it. You just deal with it. Now I told you from the gate how we got down and now you have had a chance to see for yourself. So quit ya fucking crying and finish twisting our wigs up so we can tear the club up tonight." Monica stated, calling herself checking me.

I just rolled my eyes and continued working, thinking to myself "What have I gotten myself into?"

TROUBLE IN PARADISE

Ladies and gentlemen we are now arriving in beautiful Miami Florida. The time now is 9:48am and the temperature is a warm 78 degrees. Please re-adjust your tray tables and bring your seats back to the upright position. We hope you enjoyed the flight and we thank you for flying American Airlines.

As a surprise to me Travon had flown me to Miami for a few days. After all the bullshit that went down at the shop, he knew that I desperately needed to get away. I looked over at him as he slept quietly on my shoulder. Poor thing was tired as a dog, he had been out all night doing his producing and promoting thing and didn't get home until around 4am, and we had to be at the airport at 6am.I almost felt bad waking him up but the plane was landing. He could rest once we got to the hotel.

"Baby wake up. We're here." I said, nudging him slightly. He was so tired he didn't even budge.

"Come on Tray, the plane is landing." I said, nudging him a bit harder this time.

"Okay, okay I'm up baby." He finally responded.

His eyes stayed closed but at least he wasn't in a dead sleep. Me on the other hand, I was excited as hell. I had never really been anywhere before. And as the plane descended and I saw the beautiful scenery with the ocean and palm trees I knew I was in for a good vacation. When we got outside of the airport, there was a chauffeur holding up a sign with Travon's name on it. But he wasn't standing in front of a limousine; it was a large exotic looking car. At the time I didn't know what it was, but it was black with dark tint, the back

A Gangster's Melody 137

seat windows had curtains and the emblem on the hood looked like two letter M's going through each other.

"Your chariot awaits." Travon said, pointing towards the luxury vehicle in front of us. Bu as we attempted to enter, the chauffer (who just happened to be white) stepped in front of us.

"Excuse me but this vehicle is reserved." He said, as he rolled his eyes, turned up his nose and stopped me by lightly grabbing my arm. Before I could react, Travon sprung into action.

"First of all motherfucker, take your hands off of my wife before I slap the dog shit out of you. Second of all, this car is reserved for me. Now put the luggage in the trunk before I call your boss Scott right now and have you driving yellow taxi's in New York by tomorrow." Travon said, through clenched teeth, now almost chest to chest with the chauffer. His voice was monotone yet firm and the words cut through the chauffer like a hot knife through butter.

"I-I apologize Mr. Outlaw. I h-h-had no idea sir." The chauffer said, stuttering and fumbling with the bags.

"Yeah, I know you didn't you racist motherfucker." Travon replied his voice still firm and his stare was as cold as a gangster's soul.

In all the time I had known him I had never saw Travon angry. I mean like I said, he wasn't flipping out, but his demeanor during this ordeal was a side of him that I had never seen. But even so, I decided to just write it off. After all, the man did put his hands on his wife. I melted like butter when I heard that. He had never addressed me as his wife before. God I love this man.

When we reached the Hotel it looked like it was never ending. I damn near got a crook in my neck from looking up.

"Damn baby. What floor are we staying on?" I asked, excitedly.

"We are all the way at the top. We are staying in the Penthouse suite baby." He replied, giving me a hug and a short but sensual kiss.

"Will that be all Mr. Outlaw sir?" The Chauffer said, now with a total change of attitude.

"That's all for now. But I paid to have this car on call 24 hours a day during my stay in Miami and I plan on tipping my driver very well." Travon responded, digging into his pockets while the chauffer's mouth started to water.

"Too bad the driver ain't you. Here, give Scott my card and tell him to send me a new driver." Travon said as he passed his card to the now infuriated driver.

"Mr. Outlaw that won't be necessary. I assure you that what happened at the airport was a horrible mistake and it won't happen again sir." The chauffer pleaded.

"You're damn right it won't happen again. Now beat it. Kick rocks motherfucker, before I lose my temper." Travon demanded, as the now beet red chauffer handed the bags to the bellboy who was beet red himself trying not to double over with laughter.

"Very well sir." The chauffer said, finally giving up.

The Hotel lobby was just as big and beautiful as the outside. It was decorated with a gold and cream décor, and there were very big chandeliers hanging from the ceilings. There was a large ivory piano in the center of the floor and a man in a tuxedo taking request from any guest that had one.

A Gangster's Melody   139

"I bet you don't know any Jay-Z." Travon said, ignorantly as he placed a crisp 100 dollar bill inside the man's tip cup.

The man pretended to find it funny as he accepted the money and gave a fake smile. Once we registered at the front desk we were instructed to head over to the golden elevator to the left that was separate from the rest of the elevators in the hotel. When the elevator opened up there was a man inside with a red suit on sitting on a stool, it became apparent that his job was to operate the elevator. The only thing is the elevator had no buttons; it only had a key slot that was marked PH. I'm guessing that it stood for Penthouse. When the doors closed the attendant inserted the key and the elevator began to rise. It seemed like we were headed upward forever and a day before the elevator finally came to a stop. When the doors opened we were in the living room of the biggest hotel room I had ever seen in my life. The suite was the size of three apartments. It had two floors that you accessed by climbing a winding staircase. There was a large plasma television that hung over the fireplace. There was a balcony that overlooked the whole Miami skyline as well as the beach. On the balcony there was a Jacuzzi and a wet bar. The first floor also had its own private kitchen. Upstairs there was a king size bed along with a bathroom that had another Jacuzzi as well as two stand up showers that had multiple shower heads that came out of the walls. I would find out later that it was for water massage purposes.

"So do you like it baby?" Travon asked, wrapping his arms around me and placing a nice soft kiss on my neck.

"Oh, I love it Tray, I responded.

"Well that's good because I want you to really enjoy this weekend."

"Don't worry, I'm sure I will. There is no doubt in my mind about that." I replied, closing my eyes and praying that I wasn't dreaming.

BUSINESS AND PLEASURE

It was day three of our vacation; I had just finished dicking Tiffany down and decided to handle a little business while she was asleep. D-Boy had a line on a new connect out here in Miami where I could get my shit 100% better and 20% cheaper. So besides the fact that I wanted to do something nice for Tiffany, I was also out here for business purposes. Sometimes I wish I didn't have to hide who I was or what I did, but she wasn't built for this lifestyle and would never be able to handle it. I grabbed my cell phone and called D-Boy so I could find out exactly where to meet this connect.

"Yo what's good lover boy?" D-Boy answered, knowing it was me.

"Yeah whatever nigga, what's poppin?"

"Ain't shit son, just maintaining keepin' shit in order for you while you're gone."

"That's what's up, a'ight so listen. How do I contact this nigga out here?"

"Look man, I wanted to talk to you about that. I ain't really feelin' you handling this out there by yourself, with no muscle or nothing. Do you even got a hammer with you?" D-boy asked, concerned.

"Nah not yet, but I'll handle that. You know I don't go into a situation with blinders on nigga," I responded.

"Yeah Tray, I know but I still don't see why you ain't let me and L.V. come with you to hold you down."

"Because fam, me and Tiffany are on vacation. And if she found out that ya'll were out here she would definitely know something was up. And we both know that can't happen."

"Yo. I still don't see what the big secret is. Why don't you just tell her everything?"

"Because I keep telling you, she's different. She's not like the rest of the chicks out there."

"Yeah whatever nigga. When are you going to learn? They are all the same. As long as the money is flowing they could care less about where it comes from." D-Boy stated.

"Yeah well, I ain't gonna knock your opinion, but back to business where do I meet this nigga at?"

"Okay. His name is Rodrigo. And you can meet him at his bar on Collins Ave. it's called the Oasis. Go to the back and spit your name. They expecting you."

"A'ight that's what's up. I will call you when everything is done. I'm on my way to Tracy's hotel room to pick her and the buy money up."

"One last question. How did you manage to keep Tracy a secret if ya'll was on the same flight?"

"Easy. Me and Tiffany were in first class and Tracy was in coach."

"Damn you are one smooth nigga Tray. I know you gonna tear that up while you're out there."

"Nah son I'm good. I'm out here with Tiffany. And that's what it is. I ain't even gonna play her like that."

"Yo. You kill me. I really don't understand your logic and way of thinking sometimes. Anyway, be careful nigga. And hit me as soon as that shit is done."

"You already know."

"A'ight 100."

After I hung up the phone I headed downstairs to the Maybach that I had rented for the week. After that bullshit with the first driver Scott sent me over a driver that was more to my liking. He was a young black cat named Terrence. He knew Miami like the back of his

A Gangster's Melody

143

hand, both the good and the bad. He had driven for me when I came out here, and I actually requested him originally but it was his day off. I called and let him know I was in town and what I needed and it was on. I definitely needed him around. When I got to the car he was reading the latest Don Diva magazine. When he saw me coming he put the book away and immediately got out to open my door.

"Good morning Mr. Outlaw." He greeted me.

"Hey what's up Terrence?" I asked, giving him dap.

Nothing much sir just ready to get the day started." He responded.

"Well let's do it then and oh yeah. You seem like a pretty cool dude. So from now on just call me Tray."

"Ok that's what's up Tray. And that package you requested is waiting for you. Just hit 3393# on the arm console in the back."

"Good looking Terrence." I said, before handing him $200

I got in the back of the car as Terrence closed the door. I immediately hit the code on the middle console and recovered the black .380 with the silencer attached that Terrance had stashed for me. And just as I had ordered there was no visible serial number.

"Where to Tray?" Terrence asked, through the intercom.

"First stop is the Sheraton, and then to the Oasis on Collins." I responded.

"Okay no problem." He responded, as we pulled away from the curb.

I called Tracy to tell her I was on my way and to be ready, so that we could get this business over with as soon as possible. When I arrived at the hotel I noticed that she was not standing outside as I directed her to, which was odd because Tracy always followed my orders to the letter. I was going to call her and spaz on

144 *Sean Wright*

her but when I did I was sent to the voice mail. After three re-dials I decided to go upstairs. I took the elevator to the 15th floor and proceeded to room 1527. As I approached the room I could hear slow music playing which was probably the reason she didn't hear the phone. I knocked on the door and she answered from the other side.

"Who is it?"

"It ain't fuckin' room service Tracy. Open the fucin' door." I said, upset that she wasn't ready.

When she opened the door she had absolutely nothing on. I was mesmerized for a split second as her naked body and her perfectly shaped ass sashayed over to the bed where her clothes were laid out.

"I'm sorry daddy. I know I should have been ready. But you know how us women are." She said, trying to smooth me over.

"Yeah well fuck that. You ain't getting ready for no date. You about to go and handle business. Now hurry the fuck up. Time is money. And right now you don't have either." I said, firmly letting her know that this was not a game.

"Come on baby don't be mad. You know I would never do anything to fuck your business up. You know I'm gonna always hold you down." She replied, seductively while grabbing my face with one hand and fingering herself slightly with the other.

"Girl ain't nobody got time for that shit." I barked pushing her and away.

"Okay daddy damn. Well how about when we get back?" She responded.

"Nah, it ain't even goin down like that. You're here for one purpose and one purpose only. So don't get it twisted." I reminded her. As I unzipped the secret compartment in her Louis Vitton suitcase and removed

A Gangster's Melody 145

$50,000.00 in cash, and placed it in a smaller Louis bag that I already had waiting.

"Is it because of that square bitch you got back at the hotel? Don't tell me you're actually digging that green bitch." She antagonized, as she got dressed.

"Bitch just get dressed." I barked, through clenched teeth.

She continued to mumble under her breath but I didn't give a fuck, just as long as she was getting dressed. Then I heard the comment that I had to address swiftly.

"This nigga trippin'. He gonna turn me down for that bitch? I look ten times better than her. She probably can't even fuck. *I personally think he's going faggot, wait till I tell niggas in the hood.*"

That last comment was what landed her on the floor from a vicious slap to the face.

"Would a faggot do that? Now get ya' hoe ass up and let's go." I ordered, as she complied holding her face. Tracy and I had history so she knew how I felt about the disrespect. And she let it be known as she picked herself up off the floor and grabbed her purse.

"I'm sorry daddy. I know I was way out of pocket. Trust me it won't happen again." She said, as she kissed me softly on my cheek and headed for the door.

When we got downstairs Terrance was standing outside of the car so he could let us in. when we got in I asked him to roll up the privacy glass and then I disconnected the intercom so that he could not hear what I was about to tell Tracy.

"Okay look ma. When we get in there just hold tight while I do all the talking. Don't say a fuckin' word. Just stand there and look sexy as usual. If all goes according to plan we will be in and out in no time." I instructed her.

146 *Sean Wright*

"And if all doesn't go well Tray?" She asked, already knowing the answer.

"Then it's business as usual," I said, handing her the .380.

"Not a problem daddy. You know I got you." She said as she placed the gun in her Hermes purse.

Tracy was thorough as fuck. She was by far one of the prettiest bitches I had ever come across. She was about 5'8, dark chocolate skin. About a size 7 in the waist and a 38d in the breast. Her eyes were a natural shade of green and her hair came to the middle of her back and that too was natural. So to the human eye she looked like your normal flawless model type of chick. But looks can be deceiving and that's why I stopped fucking her and put her on the team. Quiet as it is kept Tracy was the true meaning of a gangster bitch she was surgical with a stra'ight razor and definitely had no problems busting her gun. And because she was so fucking beautiful, none of the marks ever saw it coming. Her beauty always caught them off guard. Next thing they knew they were hanging with Biggie and Pac. I turned the intercom back on and instructed Terrance to head over to The Oasis.

When we arrived at the bar I instructed Terrance to keep the car running because we would be right back. Once we got inside we headed stra'ight to the back just like D-Boy said. There was an office near the bathroom and a huge bodyguard stood watch outside. As we approached, naturally he stopped us and asked us our business. I informed the dude of who I was and who I wanted to see. Rodrigo was expecting me so he just proceeded to pat us down. Finding nothing on me he then turned his attention to Tracy. And just like many times before, this so called bodyguard was stuck. It's like she had him in a trance as she stood there in her form fitting Vera Wang dress that accentuated her per-

A Gangster's Melody   147

fect shape, and her 5 inch stilettos. He was so worried about patting her down that he never even checked her purse. As usual he fell victim to the beauty. Maybe if he didn't spend so much time grabbing her ass and titties he would have been on point enough to search her purse. After the extended search, he opened the door and let us in.

"Welcome Mr. Outlaw." Rodrigo said, as he stood up from behind his marble desk.

He was small in stature; maybe about 5'5 with a medium build. He had a full goatee and his eyes were a glazed shade of blue. I'm guessing blue was his natural color and the glaze came from his personal stash of coke that was spread out on his desk.

"Please sit down have a drink or do a few lines." He insisted, all geeked up.

"No thanks. I've got a busy schedule. Let's just get down to business." I responded.

"Well Mr. Outlaw. In my country we take it as a sign of disrespect when our hospitality is brushed off." He replied, flicking the ashes of his Cuban cigar into the ashtray.

"Well in my country we don't socialize when we come to handle business. We get in and get out." I responded, staring him square in the eye.

"Okay, okay papi. Let's get down to business. Chu got the money?"

"You got the shit?"

Si, si. I've got just what you want. But first let me commend you on your reputation. It definitely precedes you. My sources tell me that you are the top dog in New York. And now you are rapidly expanding into the D.C. and Baltimore areas." He said, staring me right back in the eye from behind his desk.

His last comment automatically set the alarms off in my head. Because while it was evident that I was that nigga in NY. Nobody knew about my Baltimore moves. Nobody at all. I knew D- Boy was smart enough not to say anything. So how the fuck did this guala, guala motherfucker know?

"Well you're right. I am at the top of the food chain in NY. But as far as Baltimore I don't know what you're talking about." I said, lying but still clawing my mind for clues to how he knew.

"Tsk, tsk, tsk. Mr. Outlaw, lying to me is no way for us to start off our business relationship." He said, with an intense look on his face that immediately threw me into defense mode.

"Look, are we going to do business motherfucker or are we going to play Trivial Pursuit's Gangsters Edition?" I stated, a little more vocal than usual.

"Well, we have a slight problem Mr. Outlaw. You see, your movement into the Baltimore/D.C. area has caused great concern for some of my business associates. Under normal circumstances I wouldn't give two shits, but I have to intervene this time. You see, your nemesis Horse is Godfather to my son Hector and also my sister's fiancé and they are expecting a little bambino. So you see my dilemma. I cannot do business with you." He said, now standing up from his desk.

I made eye contact with Tracy and the look in her eyes said let me kill this nigga now, but the look in my eyes said chill baby not yet.

"Yo motherfucker, two things I hate wasting is money and time. And you got me wasting both. So with that being said, I'm taking my business elsewhere." I stated, furiously as I gave Tracy the head nod towards the door.

A Gangster's Melody 149

"Not so fast Mr. Outlaw. I think you have something that belongs to me. I'll be taking that buy money as a wedding present to my sister and her husband. I'm sure they will put it to good use." He said, snapping his fingers and extending his hand.

"Nigga you been smoking too much of ya' own shit. Now it's in your best interest to let me and my lady go on about our business and maybe just maybe I'll forget this whole thing happened." I said. It was then that he pulled a chrome .45 from his waistline.

"Look puto. That wasn't a request, now let's go. Give up the dinero and maybe just maybe I'll let you live." He said, pointing towards the Louis bag I had in my hand.

"Okay. We'll play it your way this time." I said, as I tossed the bag at his feet.

"A very wise decision Mr. Outlaw." He said, bending down to get the bag, but never taking his eyes or gun off of me. He quickly inspected the contents of the bag and sat it on the desk.

"Okay. Now for one more treat before this meeting is adjourned. Come here chica." He said, motioning for Tracy to come towards him. She looked at me for approval and I nodded in agreement. When she reached him he grabbed her from behind with the gun still pointing at me.

"Baby I been mesmerized by you since you first walked in. what do you say I get a taste of this chocolate in exchange for your life?" he said, kissing her neck and groping her with his free hand.

"Well I can't give it to you unless my daddy says I can give it to you." Tracy replied, seductively.

"Go ahead and give it to him, but make it fast so we can get the fuck out of here." I instructed.

"Now that's what I call good sportsmanship." Rodrigo stated, as he kept his gun on me and ran his tongue over Tracy's neck.

Tracy leaned her neck back and took it. She then leaned over and snorted a line of coke off of the desk. That only further excited Rodrigo as his eyes rolled back into his head and he took his eyes off of me for a split second. He then began to raise Tracy's dress up and bend her over the table as she moaned as if she were enjoying herself. As he unzipped his linen pants she stopped him.

"Hold on baby, let me do this right." Tracy said, as she turned around and dropped to her knees.

She continued to unzip his pants and pulled his dick out of his briefs. His eyes rolled back into his head one more time and Tracy made her move. She spit a razor blade out from under her tongue and cut his dick down the middle but the screams never left his mouth as she simultaneously pulled the .380 and fired a shot into his mouth, blowing his brains all over the Van Gogh pain'ting that hung on the wall behind him. As his lifeless body hit the floor Tracy leaned over him and spit in his face.

"Okay baby, that's enough. Grab the money and let's get the fuck out of here." I instructed.

"What about the nigga outside the door?" she asked.

"Pass me your pistol." I advised her, as she tossed it to me.

I then eased towards the door and looked through the peep hole. I was in luck, the massive body guard stood right in front of it. I put the barrel of the gun to the peephole and fired two shots through the door. Lucky for us his big ass body didn't drop to the floor. He slid down the door, not making any noise. I motioned for Tracy to grab Rodrigo's .45 and to follow

A Gangster's Melody

close behind me. I carefully stuck my head out of the door to see if this ambush gone wrong had been figured out. With no problems in sight, I grabbed Tracy around the waste and walked through the crowded bar as fast as I could without looking too conspicuous. Once outside, I hurried her into the car and gave Terrence the signal to get the fuck out of there. It was time to cut my vacation short and head back to get some get back.

ONE SHOT AT LOVE

It had been a while since I cut that bitch up in Tiffany's shop. I can tell she was still pissed behind that shit but she'll get over it eventually. And besides if that stupid ass nigga Gerard can forgive me I know my girl can. Don't get me wrong, Gerard was pissed, for all of about three days until I met with him, let him taste me and convinced him that his crazy ass wife attacked me with the razor and that I was just defending myself. His dumb ass was like putty in my hands. I was just going to dead him all together after that incident, but I figured if he fell for that story then he would fall for anything so why not go for the gusto? I had decided to jump out the window one last time and ask Gerard to buy me the new BMW X6 truck. He was really hesitant for a while. So I had to promise to give him the full package and then agree to cut my other "special friends" off and see him exclusively. I lied about both. I mean come on. What type of square bitch did he take me for? This lame ass nigga goes home to his wife and kids every night and I'm supposed to not see anyone else? What the fuck ever. But I played the game to get what I wanted.

I had received a text from him telling me to book a suite at the Sheraton and text him back with the room number. He requested that I wear this ugly ass lingerie outfit that he bought me while we were in St. Bart's last summer. He also requested that I leave the door unlocked because he would be arriving really late because he had to put the wife and kids to bed before he snuck out. But fuck it, I didn't care. I knew no matter what went down with us tonight; we were going down

A Gangster's Melody 153

to the BMW dealer first thing in the morning whether he wanted to or not. I could just see my fine ass stuntin' on everybody with my new truck. I really wanted it bad because nobody in the hood had one yet. Not even the biggest of the ballers. My thoughts were interrupted by my cell phone ringing.

"Wassup girl?" I asked, seeing that it was Monica calling.

"Ain't shit, what you doin bitch?"

"I'm just chillin', layin' back. What's good?"

"Get dressed, we going out with some of the dudes that play for the Ravens. You know I got most of them on my Facebook page."

"Damn girl, I can't make it. I'm already tied up with my new shorty I met at the car wash." I lied, not wanting to hear her mouth about still seeing Gerard.

"Car wash? Bitch you don't drive." She joked.

"Yeah I know. I was walking passed while he was getting his Benz detailed." I continued, with the lie.

"A'ight trick. Well you learned from the best. Hit me up if you ditch him early. We gonna be at the harbor."

"Okay. Will do. Talk to you later."

"Dueces." She responded, before hanging up.

I really hated lying to my girl, but if I told her that I was waiting to meet Gerard, she would have talked my ear off. Shit. She might have come down here and dragged me out of this damn hotel. Monica was a hustler but she was also the concerned mother hen. She took care of all of us. And that's why we all gravitated towards her. She held us down by any means necessary. I grabbed the remote and started flipping through the channels. I then looked over at the clock and realized it was 1:58am. What was taking this loser so long to get here? Shit, if I laid my game down right, I might be able to sneak away and go hang with Monica and them NFL niggas. A few minutes later I heard someone get off the elevator and I could hear that they were headed towards my suite. I quickly turned off the lights and the television and turned over so that I could pretend to be asleep when he came in. Maybe him getting here so late would work to my advantage. I could and would simply be too tired to perform any sexual favors for him. But as always, he could eat away all night. Besides having A1 credit and a shitload of money that's all he was good at. I heard him turn the knob and come in. I could hear him tip toeing towards the bed. It made my skin crawl to think that in a few seconds he would be all over me kissing my body and feeling me up. I just wanted it to be over. But he never made it to the bed, and I never heard the gunshot. I just felt my body on fire before I blacked out.

BACK TO REALITY

I woke up to my cell phone ringing off the hook. When I answered it Monica was crying and screaming hysterically. She told me that Terry had been shot and was in serious but stable condition at Baltimore Memorial Hospital. I started crying as well and immediately started packing my things. I had no idea where Travon was. He was gone when I woke up and he had not been answering his cell phone. I'm sure he would be upset about me wanting to cut the trip short, but hopefully we would understand that with one of my best friends clinging to dear life there was no way I could enjoy myself.

I had picked up the phone to call Travon again when I heard the key card being put in the door. As I rushed towards the door, he rushed through it.

"Pack your things baby; we have to head back home." He said, rushing past me and grabbing his luggage.

"Travon what the hell is going on?" I asked, confused as to why he wanted to leave. I was the one with the friend in the hospital.

"Tiffany, I don't have time to explain. Now baby please get packed. The plane leaves in thirty minutes." He said, before noticing my bags were already packed.

"What's going on?" he asked, now showing concern.

"Like you said baby, no time to explain. Let's just get to the airport." I responded.

Once we got on the plane, I explained everything to Travon; however, he had not yet explained anything to me about why he wanted to leave. He just kept saying that something happened with the boys and it required his immediate attention. He promised to make it up to me and I knew he would. When we landed D-boy and L.V. were waiting on the runway in Travon's Porsche truck. There was also a black stretch Limo waiting. Travon instructed me to take the Limo wherever I needed to go and that he would ride with the boys and meet up with me later. I kissed him good-bye and immediately headed to the hospital.

When I arrived Monica and LaShawn were at Terry's bedside. She was unconscious and hooked up to all of these machines. Monica and LaShawn looked like pure shit, like they hadn't slept in days. Their eyes were swollen and their makeup was smeared from all of the constant crying. I tried to gather myself as I approached my girls.

"Hey ya'll. What's up?" I asked, sort of chipper. Trying to lighten the mood.

"Yo they fucked her up Tiffany." LaShawn said, hugging me and crying.

"C'mon girl don't cry, she's gonna be just fine." I said patting her back and trying to sound re-assuring.

"No she ain't. Doctors say she only got a 20% chance of pulling through." Monica stated softly, staring straight ahead not really looking at anyone.

"Well Monica 20% is better than nothing. We have got to think positive." I replied, trying to keep the spirits up in the room.

"Yeah? Well yesterday she had 50% chance. So you tell me. What's so fuckin' positive about that? I swear to god, somebody's going to pay for this. Anybody whoever hated on us or ever looked at her wrong is gonna get it." Monica said, crying through clenched teeth. Still staring into space.

"C'mon Monica. We don't even know who did it, and the truth of the matter is everybody hates on us. So are we gonna go crazy on the entire city of Baltimore?"

A Gangster's Melody

I asked, trying to calm her down and talk some sense into her but she wasn't buying it.

"Look Tiffany, I'm gonna tell you again that being one of us just don't mean getting free drinks, shopping sprees and fucking first class vacations. Now if you ain't built for the total package, I suggest you fall the fuck back and re-evaluate your affiliation. Cuz shit is about to get really funky." Monica said, now staring me down with a look that could have sliced me to shreds.

"Monica it ain't even like that, but I can see you are in no mood to rationalize with me so I'm going to head home." With that being said, I walked over to Terry, said a short silent prayer and kissed her on the forehead. I then did the same to Monica and LaShawn.

"Ya'll call me and keep me updated. I'll be back later" I said, before turning and leaving. As I approached the elevator, I wiped a tear from my eye that had been dying to fall since I got there, and thought to myself…"This shit is about to get crazy."

WELCOME BACK

"Can somebody explain to me what the fuck just happened out there? How did that shit get so fucked up?" I barked at D-boy and L.V. as we pulled away from the airport headed for one of the apartments that I kept down by the Baltimore Harbor.

"Yo Tray, I had no idea that motherfucker was connected to Horse. I checked, and double checked and nothing like that ever came up." D-boy responded, adamantly.

"I say we squad up and just go find these niggas and tear them out the frame. I'm sick of all this mystery and espionage shit. Let's just gorilla these motherfuckers, lay 'em down and get this money." L.V. said, cocking back his Glock 40.

"Easy big fella, this ain't nothing but a chess match. All we gotta do is knock off all of his pawns and shit one by one. And once the king exposes himself, check mate game over." I replied, as I contemplated my next move.

When we reached the apartment I was pleased to see that there were already 5 cars full of soldiers parked out in front. Ready to hang on my every word, and put their lives on the line as soon as I raised my hand. The truth of the matter is, the gorilla mentality was not my way of thinking. I was more of a businessman. See even though hustlers ran through my bloodline, I inherited this business. *I was away at college getting my degree in law while my dad and three older brothers ruled the streets of New York with an iron fist. Drugs, murder, prostitution, number running, you name the hustle and they had it on smash. That was until they got caught in the biggest sting in NYC history and all sentenced to life with no parole. Up until then I was always shielded* from the lifestyle that they lead, and because I had a different mother than the others no one really knew I existed. My pops said it was for my own protection. And while he pushed for me to stay in school because "somebody in the family had to be legit" as he put it, I was still shown the ropes during visits.

It was shortly after the sentences were handed down that my dad requested for me to visit him. It was then that he asked me to take over the family business. He said that even though I was doing my thing in school, I had been groomed over the years for just such an emergency. He reminded me that I had been financially set since birth and that I never needed or wanted for anything. He said he needed me to step up and take over before we lost all of our business to competitors. As much as it pained me to do so, I declined my father's wishes. I was only one semester away from receiving my Masters degree in law. Even though I declined, my pops said he understood and urged me to continue with my schooling.

A few weeks later my dad and two of my brothers were killed in a prison riot between my dad's crew and a rival crew that he and my brothers had put out of business. At the funeral my mom's approached me and whispered into my ear as she hugged me. "It's your time baby; don't let your father down."

Once we got into the apartment I quieted everybody down. They sounded like an angry mob ready to torch the village.

"Okay, everybody quiet down. Let's bring this meeting to order." I stated as they immediately came to a dead silence.

"Now trust me, nobody is more heated about this latest situation than I am. And as bad as I want to just mash on these motherfuckers, we gotta do it strategically. Now remember, we are in stealth mode. Nobody really knows who we are. It's hard to fight an enemy that you can't see and I want to keep it that way for a

A Gangster's Melody 161

minute." I explained, pacing back and forth to the crowd of 20 men.

"I'm saying though" Phil blurted out, before being cut off by D-Boy.

"Nigga the floor ain't recognize you. You know the motherfuckin drill." D-Boy said, shooting Phil a cold stare.

"Permission to speak?" Phil stated, now raising his hand.

"Go ahead nigga." D-Boy replied.

"I'm sayin though. How much longer we gotta tap dance around these niggas? I came out here to lay my murder game down for the family and ya'll got my guns on safety. What's up with that?" Phil asked, as the rest of the soldiers looked on in amazement. D-Boy looked as if he was about to jump all in Phil's shit until I beat him to it by slapping him viciously across the face splattering blood from his nose.

"Now because you new to the crew I'm gonna give you a pass just this once and let you live. But as long as you live don't you ever question my authority or my tactics. Understand motherfucker?" I spoke calmly, yet firmly as Kevin raised his hand.

"The floor recognizes Kevin" D-Boy stated.

"What's the next move boss? I've been down long enough to know that you are a mastermind at this shit." Kevin said, taking a cheap shot at Phil.

"The plan is simple; as I was explaining to your captains. We play chess with them. Take out Horse's pawns one at a time and then when the king shows his head, we cut the motherfucker off." I re-iterated, to those that weren't in the original conversation with me and my captains.

"But boss, with all due respect, we don't know what this cat looks like either." Kevin responded.

162   *Sean Wright*

"Like I said, don't worry. Once we interrupt the natural order of things around here, he will slip up and show his face. And when he does, we will be there to shoot it off. Now what I want each of you to do is shake that NY swagger off. I want you to be able to blend in with your environment. So take off the Yankee fitteds, timbs, anything that says you are from up top. I want ya'll to start dressing, looking and sounding like these corny ass niggas. This is where the game gets interesting. Now ya'll go on back to ya hotel rooms and wait on further instructions from your captains."

As my army started to disperse they all came by and gave me dap and re-assured me that they were willing to die for both me and the cause. I instructed D-Boy and L.V. to stick around so I could pretty much re-iterate the game plan.

"Okay, so ya'll understand the instructions right?" I asked, already knowing the answer.

"Yeah fam'. No doubt. You know we got this shit covered." D-Boy responded.

"A'ight then, ya'll go and make sure everyone fully understands not to make a move unless they get the green light from you, and you won't move until you get it from me. Hit me later." I said, dapping them up as I walked them to the door.

"Yo Tray." D-Boy said, as he stopped suddenly and turned to me.

"What's good?"

"We gonna win this!"

"Oh nigga, I already know." I said, hugging him and closing the door. It was time to become the chess master.

HOME SWEET HOME

When I got home I noticed that Travon was still out with the guys. I wish I knew what was going on with him and what his reasons were for cutting the trip short. I would definitely find out later. But right now I just wanted to soak in a nice hot bath and gather my thoughts. I took my bag upstairs to my bedroom. I then entered my walk in closet and pulled out my pink and white terry cloth Versace pajama set with matching slippers. After that was laid out on my bed, I walked over to the wet bar that we had in the bedroom and poured myself a glass of wine, then entered the master bathroom and began to run the Jacuzzi. I set the digital control to my desired temperature, slipped off my clothes, wrapped my hair up in a towel and eased down into the steaming hot water.

As I sipped on my glass of wine I tried to make sense out of everything that was going on around me, from meeting Travon and the girls to the sequence of events that lead up to me being sprawled out ass naked in this 15 thousand dollar Italian marble Jacuzzi. I continued to sip my wine and figured I could either look at my situation as being extremely lucky or I was getting in way over my head. I mean I was happy and blessed to be living the lifestyle I was living. The money, clothes, and cars were great, and my salons were doing extremely well. But on the flip side, Travon was always away on business and Monica and the girls were proving to a bit more than I anticipated. I wished that my parents were here to guide me through this. I even wished that Mama Belle and I were able to get along. It was times like this that I really needed family to talk to. And although we had emotionally written each other off, I still sent her a check for $1,000.00 every month, because my father would have wanted it that way. And even though she cashed them faithfully without even saying thank you I still continued to send the money because I know she needed it.

My thoughts were interrupted by the sight of Travon's Porsche truck pulling up to the electronic gate on the video monitor. I was glad he was home because I wanted to fill him in on Terry's condition and to find out what was going on with him and the boys. So I quickly got out of the Jacuzzi, dried myself off, put on my outfit and headed downstairs. I got downstairs just in time to see Travon walk through the door. I immediately panicked when I noticed his white Sean John button up splattered with blood.

"Oh my God baby what happened? Are you okay?" I asked, running towards him and thoroughly expecting him for wounds.

"Calm down baby girl, I'm good." He said, just as smooth and calm as ever, while kissing me on my forehead.

"Then what happened Travon?" I asked still searching his body subconsciously.

"It ain't nothing baby. I just had a scuffle with this guy who was supposed to press up the mix tapes for us that's all." He replied, as if it were no big deal.

"A scuffle? Travon what the hell happened?" I asked, now agitated at the fact that he would involve himself in something so stupid.

"Look Tiffany, I gave these niggas 20 thousand dollars to press up these CD's and DVD's. They wanted to play with my money, so I had to fly back early and show them that it wasn't going down like that." He said, firmly.

"Travon you are too old and way too successful to be out there fighting like one of these stupid ass gang

A Gangster's Melody 165

banging drug dealers." I snapped, scolding him for behaving in such a ridiculous manner.

"Excuse me? Yo Tiffany, you have no idea what you are talking about. Didn't you hear me say I gave this motherfucker 20 G's? I keep telling you that you ain't in the backwoods of Ohio no more. Shit is real out here and you fucking with a real nigga. So please get used to it. Damn. We been together for how long now? We shouldn't even be having this talk." He snapped, back in a tone that I never heard before.

I decided not to be combative. Instead I removed his shirt, threw it in the trash and stormed off into the den to do some reading. I had just bought a copy of Sean Wright's new book. His shit always relaxed me.

After about an hour or so of reading, I decided to go shopping to take my mind off of all of the bullshit that was going on. I went upstairs and put on my black BCBG sweat suit and my black Gucci sneakers. I put my hair in a ponytail and called it a day. In the midst of getting myself together, I noticed that Travon was gone again. Oh well I had too much on my mind to be stressed out over small things. I grabbed the keys to the Mercedes S-600 off the key ring and headed to the garage. Once I pulled out of the garage I was suddenly overcome with the urge to call Monica to check on her. I hit the button on the steering wheel that allowed me to voice dial any phone number in my address book. "Call Monica's cell." I instructed as the state of the art vehicle followed my command.

"Hey Tiff what's up?" Monica said, answering the phone.

"Nothing much. How's our girl doing?" I asked.

"Still no change, but I guess it could be worse." She answered, solemnly.

166 *Sean Wright*

"Yeah you're right about that. Well look, I need to clear my head so I'm headed to Nieman's. You wanna come?" I offered.

"Yeah, why not? I have been at the hospital for hours. And Lashawn left a little while ago."

"Okay. Meet me at the back entrance in about fifteen minutes." I instructed.

"Give me twenty minutes I just want to say a few words to Terry before I leave."

"Not a problem. Give her a kiss for me and tell her I love her."

"Will do. See you in a few."

When Monica hung up, I hit the highway headed toward Nieman's. Suddenly out of nowhere I was overcome with grief and depression. I couldn't hold back the tears as thoughts of Terry laid up in the hospital fighting for her life ran through my mind. I prayed out loud for God to keep her safe and allow her to pull through it. But after what happened to my parents I knew that God had a plan for all of us. And if it was his will to see Terry through this then he would. Flashing lights behind me interrupted my thoughts.

"Pull the vehicle over now." The cop yelled through the loud speaker.

Before I could wonder what I did wrong, I looked at the speedometer and noticed that I was accidentally going 95mph in a 55mph zone. I pulled the car over to the shoulder and awaited further instruction from the police.

"Driver. Turn off your vehicle and drop the keys out of the window nice and slow." He continued to yell.

Now this was a bit ridiculous. All of this for speeding? But in any event I did what I was told. Once I dropped the keys out of the window, the two officers exited the car with their guns drawn. The driver ap-

A Gangster's Melody 167

proached my window with caution as his partner covered the passenger side of my Benz.

"Well what do we have here?" He said with a perverted look on his face.

"Let me see your license and registration." Officer hard ass instructed me. I handed him the documents he asked for and awaited further instructions.

"You know you were doing 95 in a 55 right?" He asked.

"Yes officer, but I didn't realize it until you were signaling for me to pull over. I apologize sir. I have a lot on my mind and wasn't really paying attention." I replied, trying to talk my way out of a ticket.

"Mmm Hmm. Step out of the car please ma'am." He instructed.

I knew that this wasn't protocol, but I did what I was told to avoid pissing this racist redneck motherfucker off. I stepped out of the car and he immediately turned me around placing my hands on top of the car.

"This car runs about $150,000.00. How does someone as young as you afford such a vehicle?" He asked sarcastically.

"I own my own business and my boyfriend is in the entertainment industry." I answered, honestly.

"Yeah that seems to be everybody's story now days. I'm gonna let you go with a warning but first I need to pat you down and make sure you don't have any weapons on you." He said, with a perverted sound in his voice.

"Excuse me officer, but in case you haven't noticed I am wearing a sweat suit. Where would I hide a weapon?" I asked, now getting agitated.

"There's no telling now a days." He said as he started the pat down, running his dirty ass hands all over my ass and tits. As he proceeded to head towards my pussy area I turned around.

168   *Sean Wright*

"Okay. Officer McCarty. That's enough." I stated firmly. Letting him know that I had read his name off of his badge.

"Okay Ms. Davis, you run along now and be mindful of the laws we have here in the city of Baltimore." He said, as he walked back towards his squad car.

Now I was really pissed. With everything else I had to deal with, this racist motherfucker just put the topping on a very fucked up morning. I got back in my car and continued on towards Macy's. Travon warned me that the city police would be on my ass every now and again because of the fancy cars that we drove. But all of our shit was legal so I had nothing to worry about. The shit was just a big inconvenience. I couldn't wait to tell Tray what happened.

I got to the mall just in time to see Monica pulling up driving somebody's silver Cadillac Escalade. I just smiled and shook my head. I parked not far from where she did as we both exited our vehicles simultaneously.

"Hey girl." I said, giving Monica a hug and a kiss noticing that she looked a whole lot better than she did earlier. I wasn't surprised though. We were going out in public, so I knew despite the circumstances that she was going to turn her swag on.

"Girl I'm just trying to hold myself together. This shit with Terry has really got me tripping. Who in their right mind would dare disrespect one of us, let alone do some shit like that? She asked, rhetorically

"Well Monica, there are a whole lot of haters out there. I mean let's be real. It's not like we walk on egg shells with anything that we do. But I tell you what. My money is on that nigga Gerard's wife. Ya'll did put it on her something terrible." I reminded her.

"Yeah well the bitch had it coming. And I thought about her too. But I checked around. She is way too

A Gangster's Melody 169

square to pull some shit like this. Anyway, I don't even want to think about that shit right now. Let's go spend a gang of money and try to enjoy the day." She responded. Grabbing my hand and walking me towards the mall like she was my mother afraid of me getting hit by a car.

As we walked through the mall we were buying things as if money were going out of style. And in a strange turn of events, this time it was me who was doing the treating. Thanks to Travon I was in possession of three platinum American Express cards and four other gold cards that I could use at my leisure. This sure was the life. Just to think that a little over a year ago I didn't have two nickels to rub together, and now look at me. My life was almost care and worry free. The only thing I was missing was my parents, but I get the feeling that they are my guardian angels smiling down on me and most likely the reason for my good fortune.

"Ooh girl look at this watch." Monica said, directing my attention to the diamond encrusted Gucci watch that was in the showcase of the Gucci store.

The watch was beautiful; it had a platinum bezel and 3 karats of crushed diamonds throughout the face. As we were admiring the watch, a saleswoman walked over.

"Good afternoon ladies, I see that you are taking notice at the newest women's timepiece designed by Gucci. Well ladies that watch retails at $8,500.00 maybe I can direct you a few stores down. There is a Guess store where I'm sure you will find timepieces a lot more in your price range."

Monica wasted no time retaliating to the insult.

"What did you just say to us bitch?" Monica screamed, ready to jump over the counter before I interjected.

"What my friend means, is we'll take two of them bitch." I said, in my most pleasant voice as I let my Gucci wallet unfold showing the seven major credit cards and I opened up the billfold showing at least two grand in all hundreds just for good measure. The saleswoman's mouth watered at the notion of the hefty commission she thought she was sure to receive from this sale.

"Why of course ma'am. And which card, I mean how would you like to pay for this?" She asked, unable to contain her greed. I was about to say sike and burst her bubble when a young African American saleswoman came over to the racist and pleaded her case.

"Miss Mary, I'm sorry I'm late I couldn't get a baby-sitter for Josh. I really apologize it won't happen again." She said, almost as if she were begging for her job.

"Yeah well, let's hope not. Babysitting issues are personal and no excuse. This is a business you know? I will deal with your tardiness issue later." The racist boss scolded her. I couldn't resist.

"Umm excuse me. I want her to handle this transaction and get full credit for it and all the commission." I said, pointing to the young black saleswoman.

"I'm sure you would, however that is not the way it works around here. I am the one who waited on you so I am the one who will handle the transaction." She stated matter of factly.

"Okay, so I'll tell you what. Watch this." I said, as I took three giant steps backwards out of the store and walked right back in.

"Excuse me miss? Can you help me?" I asked, now directing my attention to the black saleswoman. She looked to her very visibly pissed off boss for approval, who just rolled her eyes and walked off.

A Gangster's Melody   171

Monica and I both burst out laughing as I paid for the watches and gave the saleswoman a one hundred dollar tip on top of her already hefty commission. When we left the store we had so many bags that we decided to run the first load out to the car. When we got to the parking lot Monica's cell phone began to ring.

"Oh shit it's the hospital, Hello? What? Okay I'm on my way." She yelled, unable to hide her emotions.

"What, Monica what happened?" I asked, ready to cry just because she was.

"Terry took a turn for the worst; they are asking all friends and family to head to the hospital." She said, sobbing uncontrollably. I too began to cry as I hugged her.

"Let's go, I'll meet you there." I said, unable to fight back tears as we both got into our vehicles and sped through the parking lot headed to the expressway.

When we got to the hospital we both came to a screeching halt right in front and jumped out of our vehicles not caring about getting towed. We raced through the lobby and straight to the staircase with no time to wait on the elevator we took the steps two at a time until we reached the ICU ward. When we got to Terri's room our worst fears were confirmed our sister was gone. And the sad thing is with the exception of one or two family members, me, Monica, and LaShawn were the only ones there for her.

THE AFTERMATH

Back at my house Monica and I consoled each other over the loss of our dear friend. LaShawn said she was going to do some detective work to find out what happened to her. This was all becoming too overwhelming for me. First my parents, and now Terri. I did not handle death well, while Monica on the other hand, after her initial cry looked like it was back to business as usual.

"Girl, thanks for the shopping spree and definitely thank you for the watch, we gonna kill em with these shits." She said, holding the watch up to the light as the lights bounced of the diamonds like a piece of prism glass.

"Uh. No problem but how can you think about that at a time like this?" I asked, a little irritated.

"Look girl, Terri was my baby, and everybody knows that. But this is the life we chose. She ain't the first person I lost and she won't be the last. In this life either you end up like Terri, you end up like you, or you end up broke. And that's just the reality of it. The party don't stop because Terri is gone. It didn't stop when we lost Jennifer, it didn't stop when we lost Jackie, shit the list goes on. This ain't nothing new in B-more. Now around here we mourn our lost ones by celebrating their life. So tonight in Terri's honor we gonna do it up really big ya' dig?"

"I don't know Monica, this is too much to handle. Terri didn't trip and accidentally break her neck. She was murdered. Shot to death. This is serious. And now you wanna go party like it never happened? Fuck that. I ain't with it. That's all ya'll fuckin bitches think about is partying and catching the next victim for his money. Look where the fuck it got Terri. She was only 22 for

A Gangster's Melody

173

God's sake, she was only a baby." I couldn't hold back anymore and the floodgates were open tears flowed from my eyes like a leaking roof in a thunderstorm as the deaths of my parents and Terri flashed through my mind I was on the verge of having a breakdown.

"Aww baby come here." Monica said, hugging me and rocking me back and forth. "It'll be okay. Terri is in a much better place now. Truth be told, she was miserable as hell, just like the rest of us, depending on a niggas hustle skills as our source of survival. You right. The shit gets tired, the shit gets old, but it's all we got, it's all we know. Our parents, grandparents and great grandparents all lived the same way. So what the fuck are we gonna do? Nothing but try and perfect they hustle."

I'm not sure if it was the fact that I was super emotional or the fact that I was a little too tipsy from the cocktails that we just had but Monica's words were making a lot of sense. Who was I to judge their lifestyles and how they handled their business. I was fortunate enough to be raised in a two-parent home, slightly above middle class and in a place where there was hardly any violence. I had no idea what these girls have been through, now I saw things totally different. No wonder Monica was the self-proclaimed leader of the Stiletto Diva's; she was like the pied piper, leading us into a world where everything was everything. She had my attention now, more than ever. I listened to her soothing words as she held me in her arms and rocked me back in forth. Before I knew it we were embraced in a passionate kiss.

FUNNY MEETING YOU HERE

We interrupt this program for an ABC news brief. The violence continues throughout the city of Baltimore with the body count up to 15 in the past 48 hours. Sources close to police officials say there is a war being waged. Residents are urged to stay indoors as much as possible until the situation is under control...in other news.

"Damn baby that is so fucked up. I'm glad you're doing something with your life and you ain't involved in no dumb shit like that. These guys are so ignorant and stupid. Killing each other off and for what? That shit is just stupid. Leaving all these babies with no fathers. I mean these girls are just as stupid for getting wrapped up with those types of dudes." Tiffany stated, as she muted the television.

"Alright Tiffany damn. Slow up on all that preaching shit. You ain't never been from the hood so you don't know why these people act the way they do. You can't judge these people because all you know that might be their only means of survival." Travon replied, angrily.

"Aww that's bullshit. Don't give me that line about the man got his foot on they neck bullshit. So are you telling me that God forbid you stopped doing good in the music industry, that you are going to start slinging drugs like the rest of these fools?" Tiffany asked, just as angry.

"Hey, you never know." Travon answered, sarcastically.

"Well you better not because I'm fucking pregnant." Tiffany announced, almost in tears.

"What did you say?" Travon asked, in amazement.

A Gangster's Melody   175

"I said I'm pregnant Travon." Tiffany responded, smiling and crying.

"Oh shit. When did you find out?"

"I went to the doctor this morning. I had actually taken the drug store test twice yesterday but I wanted to be sure before I told you."

"Oh shit. Are you fucking kidding me?"

"Are you mad?"

"Mad? Hell no baby. Get dressed we're going out to celebrate."

"Aww Travon I love you baby."

"I love you too Tiffany."

I can't believe you gonna be my baby daddy." Tiffany said, in her best chicken head accent.

"No Tiffany. I'm going to be your child's father." Travon responded, kissing her soft

When we got to the restaurant it was nice and elegant and out of the way. Travon had taken me to some very nice places before but never to this spot. Once we were seated I ordered steak and lobster tails with a side of rice pilaf and Travon order broiled swordfish over a bed of lettuce. We passed the time talking about our new bundle of joy and before we knew it our food had arrived. My greedy ass dug right in.

"Baby this food is good. How come we never came here before?" Tiffany asked, stuffing a piece of lobster into her mouth.

"Because baby, as expensive as this place is we need to have a good reason to be here." Travon responded, wiping his mouth and sipping his glass of wine.

"Okay punk I got you. It's too expensive to take your girl to. But I bet you and your boys come here all the time." Tiffany stated.

"Only when we're celebrating something big." Travon responded.

"Whatever. Anyway where's your entourage at? We always have at least three of them with us." Tiffany asked.

"Yeah baby I know but this is a very special occasion. And I though because of that we could use some time alone. As a matter of fact I've turned my phone off." Travon said, before stopping a waiter. "Excuse me waiter."

"Yes sir, how may I help you?" The waiter responded.

"Can I have a bottle of Kristal please?" Travon requested.

"Certainy sir." The waiter responded.

"Hold on a second. What happened to the Louis the 13th that you sent to my table the night we first met?" Tiffany asked matter of factly.

"Oh that was just to impress you. I got you now so Kristal it is." Travon said.

"Boy don't make me throw this water on you." Tiffany said, raising her glass.

"Okay, okay . Calm down. Waiter I'll have a bottle of the Louise please." Travon requested.

"Excellent choice sir. I'll be right back." The waiter said.

"Yeah that's what I thought." Tiffany said, to Travon.

"That's your problem. You're too damn spoiled."

"Well you did it daddy. Blame yourself."

"Yeah I know. I'm kicking myself now." Travon joked, as the waiter returned.

"Here you go sir." The waiter said, as he started to pour two glasses.

"That's enough for her homey. But you can leave the bottle." Travon instructed.

"Damn baby. What's that all about? Tiffany asked.

A Gangster's Melody   177

"Shh. Just be quiet and raise your glass please." Travon instructed, before starting his toast. "To my baby, and my unborn baby. I love you both." He said, as the touched glasses.

"Thanks baby, but this ain't enough for me to get no buzz with." Tiffany joked.

"You're not supposed to get buzzed. It's celebratory, I'm about to be a father." Travon explained, before being tapped on the shoulder by the guy sitting behind him.

"Excuse me player. I'm not trying to be all up in your personal. But I overheard you say you're about to be a father?" Horse said.

"Yeah. Me and my lady are expecting. I just found out today." Travon replied.

Well congratulations man. My old lady just gave me they same news a few weeks ago. They call me Big H." Horse said, extending his hand.

"I'm Tray, and congratulations to you too player. Matter of fact let me gwet you a bottle of something." Travon said, shaking his hand.

"No thanks man, I don't drink, and wifey, well you know." Horse replied, rubbing her stomach.

"Well I'm going to the bathroom baby, by the way I'm Tiffany." Tiffany said, introducing herself to Horse's wife.

"Hey, I'm Joyce. Men can be so rude." Joyce responded.

"Yeah and Travon you know better." Tiffany scolded, jokingly.

"And Horse you know I don't play that rudeness." Joyce added, as Tiffany walked to the bathroom. As soon as she is out of sight Horse and Travon simultaneously pulled their weapons and placed them up against the seats they are sitting at.

"Well if it isn't big Horse." Travon said, with a sinister smile on his face.

"Nigga you are a dead man walking." Horse said, through gritted teeth.

"Really? That's not what my little homey right here says." Travon answered, referring to the gun he had pressed against the seat.

"Motherfucker do you think you're the only one with a little homey? Horse replied, cocking his hammer, also against the seat.

"Well that sounds like the hammer of a Sig Sawyer snub nose .32. me on the other hand am holding a double action Glock.40. Meaning, by the time you hit me once, provided your bullets go through this good leather here, I would have put three holes in you and at least one in your pretty bitch. Now how you want to play it nigga?" Travon asked.

"Like this motherfucker." Horse said, and then gave a low but distinctive whistle and nodded in the direction of numerous soldiers he had scattered at different tables around the restaurant. Upon hearing the whistle they each lifted up their heads and their shirts flashing weapons, and a snarl that said they were willing to kill or be killed for their boss.

"You see motherfucker, I ain't never caught slipping. Even when it looks like I am. But you on the other hand are going to have to learn that lesson in the afterlife. now let's go, outside." Horse said, nodding towards the door.

"Nah son. I ain't going nowhere. Not even you're stupid enough to pop off in front of all of these witnesses." Travon said, with a smile on his face and not seeming the least bit worried.

"Witnesses? Nigga I will blow the Popes head off in the front Pugh of the St. Patrick's Cathedral in the middle of Easter mass and won't nobody say shit. Yo'

A Gangster's Melody 179

bitch ass wasn't supposed to make it out of Miami alive. Tracy can't do shot right. She was supposed to kill Hector and then you. He was family and all but his prices just got way too high, and you are just becoming a pain in my ass. Now let's go before you make me prove my point and mess up this beautiful Corinthian leather." Horse said, raising his voice slightly through gritted teeth. It was then that D-Boy, L.V., Skillz, and Big John walked in, not aware of what's going on they headed straight for Travon's table and begin to reprimand him.

"Are you crazy? How in the fuck are we supposed to watch your back if we can't find you? It's a good thing our phones have GPS." D-Boy said, scolding Travon.

"Now ain't the time to preach, it's time to teach." Travon said, never taking his eyes off of Horse and nodding in the direction of his gun.

"What the fuck?" D-Boy said, he reached for his gun and so does everyone else in both crews. Travon and Horse both signal their boys to calm, down.

"This is Horse. And behind you scattered at different tables are his people. Skillz, Tiffany is in the bathroom, go get her and take her out the back, blame it on the paparazzi or something. Now we can't dance right now because you got us out manned and out gunned, but if you so much as bat a fucking eyelash while we're leaving, I swear on everything I love, my first three shots go into your bitched stomach and I know you don't want that." Travon said.

"Did you just threaten my unborn seed?" Horse yelled

"Under normal circumstances I would never do that. But I need a bargaining chip. Now me and my people are going to get up out of here real smooth like.

180 *Sean Wright*

But I promise you, we will dance again." Travon said, getting up slowly and keeping his gun on Joyce.

"I'm gonna see you soon nigga." Horse said, as Travon and his crew backed out cautiously. When they get outside there is an army of New York soldiers waiting .

"What is all of this?" Travon asked.

"Just a few soldiers from up top. See when I found out you was here, I knew to bring the wolves with me. Because everybody knows that nigga Horse is always here on Friday nights. You're slipping son for real. You are really fucking slipping, now go on home while we clean up out here." D-Boy said, visibly upset at Travon for allowing himself to be caught off guard.

"Nah Dee, let him go." Travon instructed.

"What? What the fuck do you mean let him go? We got that nigga right where we want him, and you want to let him go? Are you crazy?" D-Boy said, raising his voice.

"Yo man listen. He's sitting there with his pregnant wife. That's nigga s about to be a daddy. We dead him now and that baby pays for it later. Nah I can't have that on my conscience." Travon replied.

"Motherfucker, what about the soldiers we lost because of him? Damn near all of them was somebody's daddy. So please stop with this self righteous bullshit, because I ain't trying to hear it." D-Boy said, getting really upset.

"And I can only fix that financially right now, but we don't have to lose any more soldiers. Now I'm going home. You pack the boys up and do the same." Travon ordered, in a solemn voice.

"You showing weakness son." D-Boy spat.

"Nah fam. I'm showing growth, now go home." Travon responded, before selecting two soldiers to escort him home.

A Gangster's Melody 181

"Oh yeah, L.V. go take Tracy to see her mother." Travon instructed.

"Tracy's mother is dead."

"Yeah exactly" Travon said, as he got in the car.

When pulled off the rest of the soldiers start to disperse before being stopped by D-Boy.

"Where the fuck are ya'll going?" D-Boy asked, angrily.

"The boss said pack it up and go home." One soldier responded.

"Well fuck that. He's just going through something right now. I'm making an executive decision, and that nigga Horse goes tonight." D-Boy responded.

"But the boss said." The soldier tried to explain.

"First of all nigga that's *my* boss and I am *your* boss. So you take your orders from me." D-boy snapped, as the rest of the soldiers start to look at him funny.

"Look ya'll. I'm not back dooring Travon. That's been my brother since we was ten years old, and that's why I know what we are about to do is in his best interest. He'll thank me later trust me. Now ya'll take your places and strap up. When he walks out I want the block lit up like the fourth of July." D-Boy ordered.

ALL FOR YOU

"Mr. Outlaw you've got some explaining to do." Tiffany said, jokingly as Travon walked in the door.

"Baby I'm sorry. D-Boy and them pulled up while you were in the bathroom and they had a whole gang of reporters with them. The shit got kind of crazy so I had Skillz take you out the back." Travon lied.

"Oh what's wrong baby? You didn't want me to get my shine on? Tiffany joked, stroking his head as he lay across her lap seemingly exhausted.

"Don't worry baby. Once my little man is born ya'll are going to get more shine than ya'll can handle." Travon said, rubbing her stomach.

"Your little man? How do you know it's a boy?" Tiffany asked, smacking him playfully in the back of the head.

"Because that's all I know how to make." Travon blurted out.

"Excuse me, what the fuck does that mean?" Tiffany asked, pushing his head off of her lap.

"Stop tripping baby, I'm just playing." Travon said, kissing her stomach.

"Yeah nigga you better be." Tiffany said, smacking him again.

"Anyway, so we got to get one of the guest rooms and turn it ino the baby's room. We're going to have mad basketball shit, posters, hoops, a little locker with his name on it. I can't wait." Travon said, excitedly.

"Yeah baby, I can't wait either. I know we are going to be so happy. Just me you and the baby." Tiffany said.

"You know what baby? We need a vacation. Every time I go somewhere it's for business. We need to go

somewhere so we can just kick our feet up and relax."
Travon said.

"Well then let's just go baby. Anywhere I don't care.
Let's just pack up and go. As long as I'm with you it
doesn't even matter." Tiffany responded.

"OK I'll tell you what, let me tie up some loose ends
with the guys and have somebody hold them down
while I'm gone." Travon answered, sounding a little
down.

"Baby what's wrong?" Tiffany asked, noticing Travon's sudden mood change.

"I'm just thinking baby that's all." He responded.

"About what?"

"About retiring. I mean I got more than enough
money saved up."

"Yeah punk, I know you're caked up."

"Nah baby, you don't even understand. I'm sitting
on major, major paper. I'm talking about never have to
work another day in your life paper."

"Oh really? You been holding out Tray?"

"Something like that, but trust me it was for your
own good."

"I feel you baby, but does D-Boy and them know
you ain't gonna manage them no more? What are they
going to say?"

"Trust me baby. I've made them a hell of a lot of
money over the years. And I'm going to give the whole
crew a nice piece of the pie. Sort of like a severance
pay. That's the least I can do. I love them niggas like
brothers. As a matter of fact, they are my brothers."

"And you're giving all of this up for me?'

"Well for you and the baby mainly, but also because
I'm tired of the stress, tired of having to look over my
shoulder when I go places, having to have bodyguards
and shit." Travon said, off into his own world really
thinking about the game and not the music business.

A Gangster's Melody 185

"Damn boo, I didn't know the music business was that hectic." Tiffany said, snapping him out of it.

"Oh yeah baby. The shit is crazy and I'm tired of it."

"Well as far as us never working again, I don't want to give up the salons."

"And you don't have to. Just have somebody else run the day to day operations. We'll talk about it in the morning over breakfast." Travon said, turning the light out.

"Okay baby good night. I love you."

"I love you too baby."

EXECUTIVE DECISION

"What the fuck is taking this dude so long to bring the fucking car around? Don't he know it's a fucking war going on?" Horse said, while he and Joyce stood outside of the restaurant surrounded by security.

"Okay when I give the word light them motherfuckers up." D-boy said, speaking into his cell phone from an old hooptie sitting across the street. He watched and waited for the right time to strike and then gave the signal. "Go. Now. Now" he screamed ordering the execution. It was at that point that against Travon's wishes, his soldiers swarm out of everywhere catching Horse and his men by surprise. Horse's soldiers drop one by one and within a matter of seconds only Horse and Joyce are left holding each other in fear. As D-boy approaches Horse instinctively reaches for his gun.

"Uh uh uh playboy. Don't be no fool. Throw the ratchet down nice and slow. D-Boy ordered, cocking his gun.

"You're making a big mistake motherfucker." Horse yelled, as he threw his gun down.

"Nah my man. You made the mistake by fucking with live niggas from Queens. Now I know where your main stash house is so give me the keys and the combination to the safe in the back and I just might give you a quick death." D-Boy said, with a sinister smile on his face.

A Gangster's Melody 187

"Fuck you. Blast if you have to bitch. I was born a "G" and I'm going to die a "G". So go ahead and squeeze that shit nigga." Horse screamed.

"Okay playboy, if you say so." D-Boy responded, putting his gun to Joyce's stomach. Causing both Horse and Joyce to scream in fear.

"Okay man okay." Horse pleaded, as police sirens are heard in the distance.

"Yo Dee let's go." L.V. said, pulling on D-Boy's arm, as the sirens are getting closer.

"You heard the man nigga let's go." D-Boy said, pulling back the hammer on his gun.

"Alright man. Just be easy. Look I got over 5 million dollars in cash and another 80 keys of coke at that house. Let me walk and it's all yours" Horse said, trying to negotiate.

"It's mine anyway pussy. Now give me the keys and the combination and hurry the fuck up." D-Boy responded, smacking him with the gun. It was then that Joyce suddenly reached into her purse causing D-Boy to instinctively shoot her in the stomach. Horse screams and tries to grab D-Boy but is shot in the chest. L.V. notices something in Joyce's hand. He bent down only to realize that it was the key with the combination engraved on the back of it that she was reaching for.

"Come on man, I got the shit let's go." L.V. said, pulling on D-Boy. They got into their cars and pull off right before the police arrive. When the police arrived, they rushed over to Horse who had somehow managed to sit up and muster up enough energy to rock Joyce's lifeless body back and forth in his arms as he sobbed uncontrollably.

"They killed my baby man. They killed my fucking baby." Horse said, screaming and crying.

"Who killed your baby? Who did this?" Williams asked, trying to calm Horse down.

"Them fucking New York niggas. And I swear to God you better catch them before I do or they are all fucking dead. Do you hear me?" Horse screamed.

"OK big feller calm down, from the looks of that chest wound you're in no condition to take the law into your own hands. And what's taking the ambulance so gotdamn long?" Johnson yelled out.

"Okay man look. I have a stash house on the corner of Greenmount and York. They're going to clean me out. They got the keys, the combination to the safe and all of the info." Horse said.

"When is this going down?" Williams asked

"I don't know man. Just catch them, they took my life away from me." Horse said, crying and kissing Joyce on the forehead, as his own life slowly eased out of his body.

"Let's get some units over there and sit on the place until they show up." Williams said, to every cop that could hear him.

IT'S GOING DOWN

"Don't leave no room unchecked. Let's get it all" D-Boy said, as they rummaged through the stash house.

"Yo man. What do you think Travon is going to say about the hit on Horse?" L.V. asked.

"He'll be tight for a minute but when he sees all of this money and product he's going to be just fine." D-Boy responded, smiling and patting L.V. on the back.

"I don't know dog. That nigga is going to be mad as fuck." L.V. reminded him.

"Yeah but we got enough shit here to retire off of." D-Boy responded.

"Alright that's everything." Skillz reported.

"Alright let's bounce" D-Boy said.

"What are we going to do with them?" Lorenzo asked pointing at the hostages tied that are up.

"Fuck them. We ain't got to worry about them. We got 80 bricks and a few million in cash. I got the feeling Tray is going to want to hit the road and never look back." D-Boy said, as he signaled for his soldiers to vacate the premises. But unbeknownst to him the streets were crawling with cops just waiting for them to exit the house. The soldier they had on lookout had already been apprehended.

"All units be advised the subjects are exiting the house now. Wait until they are all outside before we make a move. They are considered extremely armed and dangerous and we don't expect them to go quietly. Excessive force is authorized. I repeat, excessive force is authorized if necessary. Okay here they come now. There are no visible weapons, but each is carrying a large duffle bag. We will move on them when they are all inside the car. I repeat we will take them in the vehicle." Williams announced, into the walkie-talkie. As

A Gangster's Melody 191

D-Boy and the crew head for the car they look around cautiously but don't notice the cops and once inside the car Williams give the order.

"Go, go, go." Williams yells into the radio. The police swarm the vehicle with guns drawn.

"Let me see your hands."

"Don't fucking move."

SINK OR SWIM

"These New York motherfuckers are tough as nails." Williams said, after interrogating each and every member of Travon's crew.

"Yeah if they were locals we'd be home with our wives by now." Johnson replied.

"Okay. I've heard bits and pieces but what have we got?" Lt. Daniels asked.

"Well sir we've got a lot, then again we got shit." Williams answered.

"What he means sir is we got a search and seizure. 8 perps, a bunch of automatics weapons, over 5 million in cash and a shit load of coke. These boys appear to be from New York and the reason behind the majority of these bodies." Johnson replied, noticing the perplexed look on Lt. Daniels' face.

"Well that sounds like a hell of a bust to me. What's the problem? Lt. Daniels asked.

"Well sir we believe a few things, first is what we have locked up right now are just a few of the soldiers in the New York crew. From what we can tell, there is some sort of chain of command in the cell, with the guy in the yellow shirt in charge, the guy in the blue shirt not too far behind and everyone else are just soldiers." Johnson replied.

"Okay. What's your point?" Lt. Daniels asked.

"Sir the point is, these guys are very low level. If we lock them up their boss will just replace them with a new crew tomorrow. And that means more drugs, more war, and a lot more bodies." Williams responded.

"Okay so what do you suggest we do? Let them go Sergeant?" Lt. Daniels said, sarcastically.

A Gangster's Melody   193

"Not exactly sir. We find out who's in charge in there and offer them a deal to give up their boss." Williams said.

"What kind of deal are we talking about?" Lt Daniels asked.

"Well if we can get them to roll on their boss, we cut them loose." Johnson answered, hesitantly.

"Are you out of your fucking mind detective?" Lt. Daniels screamed.

"No sir. It's kind of like the snake theory." Johnson answered.

"What fucking snake?" Lt. Daniels asked, visibly upset.

"What he means sir is if you cut the head off of the snake then the body will fall. If we get them to give up their boss we take him off the grid, the war is over and our city's murder rate drops tremendously." Williams explained.

"Okay. The wheels are turning, but how do we get them to snitch? I've heard stories about those New York boys. They are thick as thieves." Lt. Daniels said.

"Let them set up the boss for total immunity. They walk right out. No tricks and no hassles." Johnson answered.

"No. No fucking way. Reduced sentences yes. Total immunity? No courtroom, no testifying, no nothing? No fucking way." Lt. Daniels said.

" LT. We tried the reduced sentence thing and they won't budge, but I'm hoping if we dangle this offer of total immunity they'll bite. I'm willing to bet that the guns we recovered will lead us back to all the recent murders since these guys have been on the scene. Now my source says that when we busted them they were on their way to deliver to the boss. The guns, coke, money and everything. I say we cut them loose, and follow them to the big man. Then have units sit on the

194   *Sean Wright*

house until the warrant is signed and take the mother-fucker down." Williams said.

"Assuming that I go for this, how do we know they will roll over on their boss? Lt. Daniels asked.

"We don't. But it's worth a try." Johnson answered.

"The major will have my badge if he finds out about this." Lt Daniels said.

"Sir with all due respect the COMSAT meetings are coming up and if this war continues and the bodies keep falling the way they are, they are going to have your badge anyway. So in that case what do you really have to lose?" Williams said.

"Okay. If we do it we do it my way. Put the offer out there to all of them. Then put them together in the think tank and let them kick the idea around and see what they come up with. As a matter of fact, I'll do it. They need to see a new face. Has any of them made a phone call yet?" Lt. Daniels asked.

"No sir and we confiscated all cell phones and PDA's at the time of arrest." Williams responded.

"OK good. But that means we only have a little bit of time before their boss knows their missing and something is wrong. We have to move fast. I'll start with the capo in there. Something tells me he's the one running the show, at least on his level. Lt. Daniels said, before entering the room where D-Boy sat calmly.

"How you doing? I'm Lt. Daniels, homicide. And you are?" Lt. Daniels stated, trying to break the ice.

"Michael fucking Jackson. Now get my lawyer and get the fuck out of my face." D-Boy answered, laughing in his face.

"Now is that anyway to talk to the person that's here to help you?" Lt. Daniels asked.

"Okay. Okay. Let me guess ya'll about to do that good cop, bad cop shit? Suck my dick nigga. I watch The First 48 faithfully." D-Boy laughed.

A Gangster's Melody 195

"Listen here motherfucker. I am the good cop and the bad cop. So sit back and listen. Now like I said, I'm from the homicide division. Which means I can give two shits about the little drug enterprise you got going on. But when bodies start falling the way they have, especially in my district, my dick gets hard and I want to raw fuck whoever's responsible. You following me Michael Jackson?" Lt. Daniels barked.

"Whatever man. Get me my fucking phone call so I can get up out of here." D-Boy said, waving him off.

"Now I know you're just one of the many pawns in the game so here is my one time offer. Point me in the direction of te boss and you walk. All of you scott free. No testimony, no court, no nothing." Lt. Daniels offered.

"Motherfucker New York soldiers don't snitch. We are true soldiers. So take that offer and shove it right up your faggot ass." D-Boy said, adamantly.

"Okay. If that's the way you want to play it. I mean for what it's worth I admire the loyalty ya'll motherfuckers got. These boys down here are weaker than the links in a fake gold chain. However, what I need to do now is put you back in the holding cell with your homies. Then I'm going to have ballistics run a check on all of that heat ya'll got caught with. Then I'm going to call my boy over in narcotics and tell him I got an early Christmas present for him. By that time the ballistics checks should be back matching your guns to at least ninety percent of the murders in the past 6 months. Then when I got enough info to put you and your people away for about ten lifetimes, I'm going to call my cousin who just happens to be the District Attorney. Meanwhile the boss you are protecting is home fucking his girl and yours too. So who's the faggot now? Let's go Mr. Loyalty." Lt. Daniels said, leading D-Boy back to the holding cell.

DECISIONS

"So they are offering us a walk on all of that shit?" Skillz asked.

"Yeah man." D-Boy said, solemnly.

"Well fuck that shit man. I ain't snitching on my man. With all that he's done for me, I'll lay down and die for that nigga. I'll take the heat for everything, guns, bodies, coke, fuck it. I'll eat it." Lorenzo said, pounding on his chest.

"Damn son, that's what's up. But we need you in these streets. Let one of these little niggas earn they stripes." L.V. said, noticing the nervous looks on the other soldiers in the cell. "Don't be looking all stupid. It's part of the game. Ya'll niggas knew this day might come. And now it's here. So who is going to step up and fall on the sword? I don't give a fuck who does it. Ya'll huddle in the corner, draw straws, pick a number, I don't give a fuck if you do paper-rock -scissors I want a name in 5 minutes. Don't make me choose." L.V. barked.

"Yo "L", Skillz, Renzo, Big John, come here for a minute. listen ya'll this is going to sound crazy really fucking crazy. But I was thinking about taking that offer man." D-Boy said, sounding a bit ashamed.

"Nigga are you crazy?" Skillz asked.

"Look man just listen. I don't like the idea no more than ya'll do. But let's be real that nigga going soft over Tiffany. He already has been hinting towards the idea of pulling out and shutting the operation down. He don't even want to give up his connection because he says if we fuck it up, it will still fall back on him. Now we all know that he is sitting on about 4 or 5 million. So he can afford to call it quits. But with him out of the game we're fucked. None of us in here got enough to

A Gangster's Melody

retire on. We all got lavish lifestyles to maintain, and Tray's pussy whipped ass is going to fuck it up for everybody and take all of that away from us. You already know this music business don't pay shit. We was just using that as a front anyway. So even if one of the young boys takes the fall we are fucked anyway. Travon is showing weakness man and fucking with him we are either going to end up dead, broke or dead broke. So as much as it kills me to say it, if we remove the weak link to the chain we can continue to get this money and feed our families." D-Boy said.

"I feel you man but Travon been our man from day one and the shit just don't seem right." Skillz said.

"That's right. And I'm only enforcing the rules and regulations that he taught us. Come on man. If it was anybody else showing weakness he'd have them put to sleep and he'd have one of us do it." D-Boy explained.

"Yeah I feel you. But if we give up Tray we are still fucked because we don't have his connect." L.V. added.

"Let me worry about that. So do we all agree that Tray has to go?" D-Boy asked.

"As much as I hate to admit it. Yeah man I have to ride with you. Like you said if it were somebody else Tray would do the same thing." Skillz concurred.

"Look man Travon is cool. I love him and the whole shit. But at the end of the day that's your man Dee. My loyalty is to you dog." L.V. responded.

"Well I'm loyal to the money so it's whatever." Big John said.

"Well I ain't feeling this shit. And I can't believe we're even talking about this shit. Ya'll are acting like he ain't been feeding us and our families in years. We ain't never been without as long as we were on Travon's team. Now ya'll want to sell him out? Nah. Ya'll ain't got my vote. I'd take a bullet for him so jail ain't shit. If I would give my life then doing life don't bother me. Fuck it." Lorenzo said, showing his loyalty. As Lt. Daniels walks up.

"Just figured I would stop by to see if you boys were playing nice." He said, sarcastically.

"Let me out. Let's talk." D-Boy said.

"Looks like you've been out voted dog. Now just sit back, chill and ride it out. Trust me. D-Boy's going to make sure we eat." L.V. told Lorenzo.

DECEPTION

"What the fuck?" Travon said, looking at the clock wondering who was at the door this time of night.

"Baby it's four in the morning. Who the hell is it?" Tiffany asked.

"I don't know but I'm about to find out, stay here." Travon said, reaching under his pillow and grabbing his gun.

"Travon what is going on?" Tiffany said, grabbing her robe.

"I don't know. Stay here Tiffany." Travon ordered, before heading downstairs cautiously with his gun in hand. He looked out the peep hole to see it's D-Boy and L.V.. he opens the door and they walk right passed him.

"Your fucking cell phone is off again." D-Boy yelled.

"D-Boy what the fuck are you doing here? Do you know what time it is?" Travon asked.

"Yeah but I've got good news. So good this shit couldn't wait." D-Boy responded.

"You're going to love us for this." L.V. stated.

"I already love ya'll but it's four in the fucking morning dog. Now what's so important that it couldn't wait another three or four hours?" Travon said.

"Tray our problems out here in Baltimore are over baby." D-Boy said, excitedly.

"What are you talking about Dee?" Travon asked, curiously.

"I fixed everything son. That nigga Horse and his people are done off. And then to put the icing on the cake we hit the main stash house nigga, 40 bricks and 2.5 million in cash. We did it son." D-Boy said, lying about the amount of drugs and money that was taken.

"What the fuck did you do Dee? I told you to leave that shit alone." Travon yelled.

"I did what you should have done. I handled business nigga. I don't know what has gotten into you. You showing weakness son. That ain't the Tray I know. And it damn sure ain't the Tray that taught me the fucking game." D-Boy yelled back.

"Since when do you run the fucking show Dee? This is my shit nigga. I make the fucking calls. I bark and you bite. That's how it's always been and that's how it is now." Travon continued yelling.

"Well what's done is done partner. So lace up your boot straps and grab your nuts because we got more work to do. And I'm going to pull your coat to something player. All that lovey dovey shit don't fly in our lifestyles and you know it. Now what's in these bags can change our lives forever. We got more product and more money than we ever expected to get from this city. So now that we've conquered Baltimore, what's next Ohio? Atlanta?" D-Boy asked.

"I'm out Dee. That's it for me. I'm out. I quit." Travon said.

"Look man, I don't think you should do that. Now I know you're mad right now but as your brother I'm begging you to reconsider." D-Boy said, softly trying to get Travon to change his mind.

"And as your brother I'm asking that you trust and respect my decision." Travon replied.

"You know what? You acting like a real bitch right now. Now man up and take charge of your army. Command your soldiers partner." D-boy said, angrily.

"Okay. Here's a command for you. Get the fuck out of my crib. Come back later when you got some fucking respect. As for the shit that's in these bags they'll be dealt with accordingly. We'll meet up later and talk about it, but for now roll the fuck out." Travon or-

A Gangster's Melody   201

dered, pointing to the door, before Tiffany comes downstairs.

"Is everything OK down here?" Tiffany asked.

"I thought I told you to stay upstairs." Travon barked, grabbing the bags and heading upstairs.

"Well I heard all of the yelling and I just wanted to make sure everything was alright." Tiffany explained.

"Next time do what the fuck I tell you to do." Travon yelled, as he continued upstairs.

"What's up Dee? What's up "L"?" She said.

"What's up Tiffany?" They both responded, with a sad look on their faces.

"What's wrong? Y'all don't look too good." Tiffany said.

"We good." D-Boy replied.

"Can I get ya'll something?" Tiffany offered.

"Nah we about to be out." L.V. responded.

"Alright then I'm about to take my black ass back to bed then. I'm sure I'll see ya'll later. Tiffany said, turning to head back upstairs.

"Hey Tiffany?" D-Boy said, stopping her.

"Yeah what's up?" She replied.

"You know how to contact me if you ever need anything right?" D-Boy asked.

"Yeah Dee. I'll just tell Travon to call you for me." She responded.

"Nah what I mean is.." D-Boy started to say, before Travon headed back downstairs.

"Why are ya'll niggas still here? Travon asked angrily.

"We're leaving now man." L.V. replied as Travon walked them to the door D-Boy turns to Travon almost with tears in his eyes.

"Yo Tray man. I'm asking again as your brother to please reconsider." D-Boy said, sadly.

"Dee my mind is made up son. And calm down it ain't that serious. Now go home and wait for my call." Travon replied, patting him on his back as he closed the door behind them. Once outside they walk to the car and L.V. addresses one of the young soldiers sitting in the back seat.

"Looks like you dodged a bullet little homey." L.V. said, before he and D-Boy got in the car and drove passed Williams and Johnson who had been sitting up the block waiting for the deal to go down. D-Boy passes and gave a head nod signaling that the mission is complete.

"Poor kid. He must feel like shit throwing his boy to the wolves like that." Johnson said, noticing the look of pain on D-Boy's face.

"Yeah well he'll feel better once he gets out of Baltimore and sets up shop somewhere else. Shit, what else can he ask for? They got their freedom, their lives, a fresh start anywhere but Baltimore and half of the drugs and money they stole from that stash house." Williams replied.

"Yeah but let him tell it Travon is like his brother. That's got to suck." Johnson said.

"Yeah well what's done is done so don't get all gay and shit on me. All units stand by for my command." Williams said, speaking into the walkie-talkie.

A WOLF IN SHEEPS CLOTHING

"I guess they didn't take it too well." Tiffany said

"Hell no. But fuck them; they'll get over it. Coming up in my crib yelling and shit" Travon responded.

"Even after you told them about the baby?" Tiffany asked.

"I ain't tell them shit. They just started flipping. I didn't get a chance to explain nothing." Travon responded.

"Well baby you knew they would be upset. You have to call them and explain why. Tell them about the money you're going to break them off with. Maybe that'll make them feel better." Tiffany said.

"Fuck that. I ain't kissing they ass."

"You and D-Boy been friends since ya'll was ten years old. Now be the bigger person and call him Tray. And I'm not asking you I'm telling you." Tiffany demanded.

"Okay Tiffany damn." Travon said, grabbing his cell and heading out of the room.

"Where are you going?"

"Downstairs for some privacy."

"Well excuse me."

"I'll be right back baby." Travon said heading downstairs and dialing D-Boy's number. The phone rings a few times and then goes to the voicemail.

"Yo Dee listen. You know I hate talking on these things so catch the slick talk. First off the reason why I have to stop playing ball is because Tiffany is pregnant. Yeah she's having my baby, and you're going to be an uncle nigga. But not only that Dee, we had a damn good run man. We got cake out the ass and we are still alive to enjoy it. And I hope ya'll wasn't thinking I was just going to bounce and leave ya'll all fucked up. I was going to wait until later but I might as well tell you now. I was going to give each captain a million as a parting gift. Ya'll been loyal brothers to me and I want to give ya'll enough to retire on and enjoy. Them streets is played out son. Spread the word. Bring everybody by tonight so ya'll can get your bread and we can plan a trip somewhere. Just remember you're my brother and I love you. Hit me later peace." Travon said, speaking into the phone.

***

"Yo man why are we sitting here?" LV. Asked, as he and D-Boy sat in the car at the end of Travon's block.

"I have to sit here and make sure they keep they word and they don't hurt Travon man." D-Boy said, sounding concerned.

"I feel you on that, but what if they do? What can you possibly do? What if they have to pop that nigga, do you really want to watch that shit go down?" L.V. said.

"I guess you're right when you put it like that. Oh shit." D-Boy responded, grabbing his vibrating cell phone.

"What's up?" L.V. asked.

"It's Travon calling." D-boy replied.

"Yo It's a wrap. Let that shit go to voicemail." L.V. said, taking the phone from D-Boy.

"Alright man, I know it's a wrap but that's still my brother in there. Before we bounce I want to at least hear the voicemail." D-Boy says, as he listens intensely to the voicemail Travon has left. As he listens to the voicemail his facial expression proves that he has made a big mistake by giving up his brother. As the voicemail comes to an end D-Boy threw his cell phone down, exits the car and started running down the block

A Gangster's Melody   205

as if he can undo what he has already done. But it's too late.

"RED TEAM GO, BLUE TEAM GO, GOLD TEAM STAND FAST." Williams yelled into the walkie-talkie, as what seems to be the entire Baltimore Police Department converge on the house. But they don't kick the door in; instead they knock on the door.

"Damn I thought I told ya'll to come back later." Travon said, answering the door thinking it was D-Boy and L.V. As soon as he opened the door the police stormed the house.

"Get down, show me your hands, don't fucking move." A few of the officers yell, as they throw Travon to the ground and handcuff him.

"Yo what the fuck is ya'll doing? Get the fuck off of me." Travon screamed, as Detective Williams and Johnson make their way into the living room and show Travon the search warrant.

"Well if it ain't the King of New York. Do you know what this is motherfucker?" Williams asked, showing him the warrant.

"Your mothers grocery list?" Travon responded, sarcastically.

"Very funny bitch. It's a search warrant. And I bet my squad car to your Bentley that I find enough shit here to send you to Death Row. And I ain't talking about cutting no record with Sugar Knight either." Williams barked back.

"I don't know what the fuck you're talking about." Travon lied, as Tiffany headed downstairs.

"Are ya'll at it again? What the.." Tiffany said, before she realized what was going on.

"Freeze. Show me your hands." An officer yelled out.

"Travon what is going on?" Tiffany asked, obviously confused.

"Get down here and show me your fucking hands." The officer yelled louder, causing a few of his partners to rush Tiffany, wrestle her to the ground and handcuff her.

"Travon what's happening? Tiffany yelled out, now starting to cry.

"Baby I don't know. Just be cool. I'm sure this is all just a misunderstanding and we are going to sue these motherfuckers for everything they got. And Tiffany just remember, no matter what happens. None of this was a lie. I do love you." Travon said, as he and Tiffany lay on the ground handcuffed facing one another. As a few cops come downstairs carrying a bunch of duffle bags.

" Jackpot. We got money, we got murder weapons, we got a shit load of cocaine. Get it while it's hot. Everything must go." One of the cops joked.

"Drugs? Murder weapons? Somebody please tell me what is going on?" Tiffany said, now fully hysterical.

"Tell her Romeo. Tell her what's going." Johnson said.

"Man I ain't never seen none of that shit in my life." Travon lied, again.

"What? Travon what are you saying? They planted that shit? Ya'll motherfuckers planted that shit?" Tiffany screamed, frantically.

"Look, I don't know what the fuck is going on? You got something you want to tell me Tiffany?" Travon said.

"Don't try and put it on her you no good motherfucker. Your boy already gave you up. You can thank D-Boy for this." Williams said.

"What? Bullshit. Ya'll some motherfucking liars. Tiffany what type of shit have you gotten me into?" Tra-

A Gangster's Melody 207

von said, now going into an Oscar winning performance.

"Travon baby please stop. This isn't funny please stop." Tiffany pleaded, now crying uncontrollably.

"I want a fucking lawyer right now. That shit ain't mines and you can't tie it to me neither. No fingerprints, no nothing. Where the fuck did ya'll find that shit huh?" Travon asked, adamantly.

"Well where did you get it?" Williams asked, the officer that brought the stuff downstairs.

"In her closet. Under the floor board." The cop replied.

"What? No. This can't be happening. Travon baby please stop. Why are you doing this to me?" Tiffany continued to plead.

"Get them both out of here. We'll clear this up downtown." Johnson said.

As the officers lead Travon and Tiffany passed the Detectives. Williams stops Travon.

"You think you are so slick don't you bitch? I'm going to personally make sure you get buried under the fucking cell, that's if you don't get the death penalty. Now get this faggot out of my sight." Williams said, as the officers lead Travon and Tiffany out to the squad car. Tiffany is understandably kicking and screaming while Travon is just as cool as always. By this time a crowd has gathered outside and Travon makes eye contact with D-Boy who is trying to fight through the barricades as if he can undo what he has done. As Travon is being put into the car he shoots D-Boy a sinister look as D-Boy looks like he just lost his best friend.

A NEW BEGINNING

"Yeah, I know ya'll mouths are hanging wide open. I couldn't believe that shit either, and I'm still finding it hard to get over. The man that I loved, the one who claimed he loved me, the nigga that fathered my child had been lying to me all of this time. Now some of you are calling me things like jackass, and naïve. Some of you hypocrites are even calling me a dumb bitch. As if what happened to me couldn't or hasn't happened to you. Shit. This type of thing happens to females like me and you every day. I'm just the only one who ain't scared to tell her story. You see I don't care if you call me a dumb bitch because I was, I'll admit it. But I'm hoping ya'll can learn from my story. Oh yeah my story. Let's get back to it....

As ya'll read, that motherfucker Travon blamed all of that shit on me, the guns, coke, money, everything. When we got down to the precinct somebody bailed him out, to the tune of $1 million dollars. I'll admit, that same someone tried to bail me out too but I was denied bail because all of that shit was tied to my name, houses, cars, jewelry, the beauty salons everything, and I had no way to show how I earned any of it. Surprisingly enough the same someone that tried to post my bail also paid for my attorney. The attorney wouldn't tell me who retained his services but I figured it was Travon. The question was did he really love me and just get caught up, or was I just a convenient piece of pussy and a scapegoat and the motherfucker just felt guilty?

In any event, against my lawyer's advice I took the case to trial. The D.A. had offered a deal of 20 years even though it was only my first offense. But I was 4

A Gangster's Melody 209

months pregnant and I was 100% innocent. I knew that I would win if I took the case to trial. Monica convinced my grandmother to testify for me, but she ended up hurting my case even more by saying that she barely knew me and that I moved out as soon as I got there. She told how I was driving expensive cars and living lavishly and hanging out with the wrong crowd. You would think that she was testifying against me. Monica and the girls couldn't even help me because their records were so fucked up that they couldn't be credible witnesses. So I was all alone. It was me against the government's star witness, Mr. Travon Outlaw. I broke down right there in my seat watching my first and only love testify against me. According to him *he* was the naïve one. He said that *I* showered *him* with money, cars and expensive gifts. He said when he asked where all of my money came from, I told him it came from owning three beauty salons. (You know, the ones he bought for me.) When I took the stand I could barely hold myself together, and Travon couldn't look me in my face. But I told my story. I told the truth. I explained how I was only guilty of being a young naïve girl from Marion Ohio who was in love, dangerously in love as the song goes. I noticed some jury members getting teary-eyed listening to my testimony. I thought I noticed Travon wipe a tear from his eye and mouth the words I'm sorry. I had won the trial; I could feel it in my heart and soul. The jury came back with its decision. The judge ordered me to stand as the jury read the verdict. GUILTY on all counts. I was hit with the 848, that was the kingpin statute. I was sentenced to 372 years in jail. I collapsed right then and there. I lost three things that day, my mind, my freedom, and my baby. Travon on the other hand left with everything, including his wife and 2 sons, from New York. Yeah that's right you read correctly. Travon was married with children. His defense team celebrated while Travon just sat there with his head in his hands looking like he just lost his best friend, because he knew that he had. So that's how it ends, with a new beginning. It's Okay to cry, go ahead. But don't cry for me, cry for the women that this is happening to everyday. If you know someone in this similar situation have them read this book and tell them that I am a diamond in the rough and I leave this jewel. All money ain't good money, because in the end he played me like a gangster's melody. Peace.

Outside of the courthouse D-Boy is parked alone and stressed about the thought of his best friend going to jail forever on the count of his disloyalty and betrayal. He is crying and very distraught when a car with tinted windows pulls up along side of him. The window rolls down and Lorenzo is driving with Travon in the passenger seat.

"What's up my brother?" Travon said, before he pulls out a gun with a silencer shoots D-Boy three times in the face and they pull off.

Printed in Great Britain
by Amazon